Clan of the LOBSTER MAN

MAUREEN O'NEILL HOOKER

 Year of the Book
135 Glen Avenue
Glen Rock, PA 17327

ISBN: 978-1-64649-398-2 (paperback)
ISBN: 978-1-64649-399-9 (ebook)

To my clan:

Germaine Joubert and James P. O'Neill

J. Barry O'Neill

James Stewart Hooker

Tamara Hooker and Robert Wolbert,
Joseph Patrick, and Jennifer Lucille Hooker

Ryan James Wolbert and Andrew Robert Wolbert

The Petrillos

The O'Learys

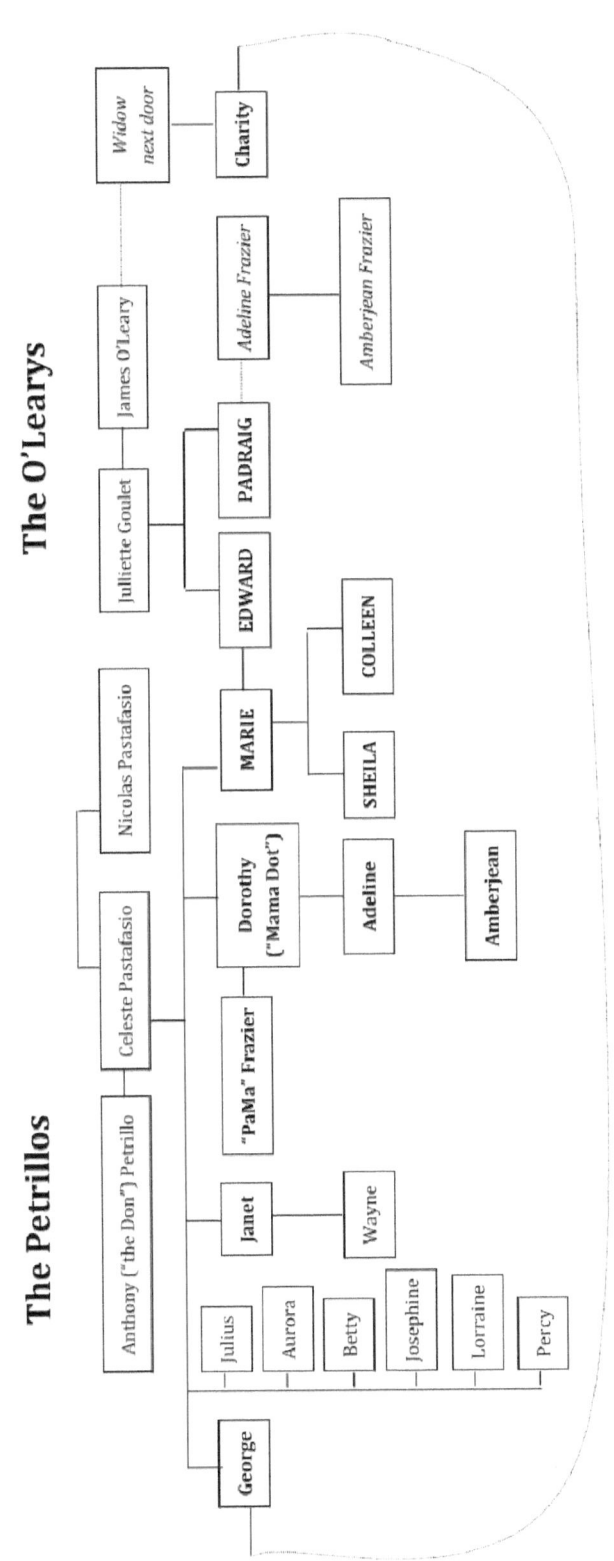

Contents

1 | Colleen and Sheila 1

2 | Edward and Marie.. 7

3 | Marie and Edward..25

4 | Uncle Nick and Colleen...37

5 | Padraig 49

6 | Adeline 59

7 | Charity..77

8 | Colleen..93

9 | Wilson... 109

10 | Keith... 119

11 | Adeline and Amberjean 133

12 | November 22, 1963... 145

13 | Cambridge 167

14 | Wilson... 181

15 | Padraig's Funeral...199

1 Colleen and Sheila

Colleen returned the stare of a glassy-eyed fish while her father's lobster boat rocked in heavy swells. Edward O'Leary's traps were baited and stacked on the stern. The motor roared, and the Gray Gull heaved up and down like an old lady trying to get out of a chair.

Six feet to a fathom, twenty fathoms between traps, ten traps to a trawl, the wooden lobster traps were water-logged, weighted with old bricks, connected by twisted rope, hairy with seaweed. After the first was pushed overboard, the others followed like synchronized swimmers, while the rope between them pulled tight.

Edward had never heard of anyone saving himself after being caught in the rope, but he kept a knife in his pocket as though cutting himself free was an option. In truth, he would be helpless before he hit the water. Still, he could not face the sea without the knife.

On their way to St. Clair's Nursery School, his daughters Colleen and Sheila observed the traps as they disappeared in a splash. The twins knew to stay clear of the ropes, that they would be gone before they could scream. Not that a scream would be heard over the clamor.

The nuns would not permit girls to wear slacks to school. Their mother, Marie, made the warm overalls they wore under dresses of black watch plaid. She knitted their sweaters, and even made the jackets they wore when it was bitter cold. Marie could make anything, and she had a sharp eye for cheap remnants. On Saturday she dragged the wringer washer from the common stairway at the back door, to the kitchen sink. Too tired to heat hot water and bleach, she pretended not to hear the persnickety neighbor who muttered about the dullness of her whites.

They lived close to the water, where things were always damp. It took the better part of a day for laundry to dry. Children played hide and seek, running through rows of flapping sheets, and touching them with dirty fingers. Some mothers had a fit. Colleen and Sheila were glad that their mother didn't interrupt their games.

On Saturday the girls took a bath and washed their hair. Dipping under the shallow water as it turned from clear to cloudy, they continually asked Marie for more hot water, saying that it was barely warm. Their mother carried steaming pans from the stove to the tub until her arms trembled. In summer they splashed a long time, but in winter, shivering forced them to leave the tub quickly. Marie welcomed them into pajamas warmed on the top of the kerosene heater.

Whatever the weather, they sat on the floor in front of their huge radio before bedtime. While Marie ironed and mended, the Lone Ranger and his trusty sidekick, Tonto, kept law-abiding citizens safe.

The girls had thick dark chestnut hair parted in the middle and braided when Marie had time. Straight bangs framed their freckled faces and hazel eyes. They were taller than most girls their age, long-legged, skinny, and the only twins in their extended family, their school, their church, or their neighborhood. Twins were unusual in 1947.

Edward took Marie and the girls to the wharf where he dropped lobsters into a burlap sack for the nuns. Their mother held their hands and walked them up the hill to St. Clair's Nursery School, where she gave the lobsters to the nuns in payment for childcare, before returning to the wharf and her job on the electric switch assembly line at the Monowatt Plant.

Sister Yvonne, in a wimple later made famous by the flying nun, lined the children up to give them a spoonful of cod liver oil, followed by molasses. After they licked the spoon clean, Sister Yvonne filled it again, and passed it to the next child. In the afternoon, they filled mason jars with Japanese beetles pulled from the convent rose

2

bushes. Although the jars were never full, Sister Yvonne gave them a cookie anyway.

At the end of her shift, Marie O'Leary returned for Colleen and Sheila. There was no boat ride in the afternoon. If Edward had caught anything, he would already have sold it, and gone to Leo's First and Last Stop to talk to a man about a horse.

On harbor boat tours these days, a guide points to the old stone building and explains that it was the first project of Alexander McGregor's Irish laborers after they finished Fort Adams. Shops on the ground level sell an assortment of tee shirts and useless souvenirs. Even old sweatshops are gentrified in Newport, Rhode Island.

Colleen and Sheila had been halves of the same ovum twirling around each other before they had gills; they swam in the same amniotic fluid, in the same placental sac. Despite the threat of getting tangled in each other's umbilical cords, they cohabitated safely, for thirty-two weeks.

From the day they were born, they communicated with each other through gestures, sounds, and touches. Even when she wasn't paying attention, Marie noticed that when one of the babies cried, she turned first to her sister for soothing.

A doctor who saw the girls called their speech "Idioglossia" and told Marie that having their own language should be forbidden. He pointed out that reading and writing would be hard to learn, if the girls spoke a language the teacher wasn't teaching, and did not understand.

Marie explained it to them the way the doctor had. She told the girls they had to stop speaking as they did, because it wasn't allowed at the "big-girls" school. Colleen refused, but Sheila wanted to do well in school, and when she heard what the doctor said, she stopped immediately. Afterwards, if Colleen spoke in their language, Sheila would not respond. Even when Colleen was standing right beside her, the door to Sheila was shut.

Colleen persisted, and one morning, while getting dressed, Sheila had had enough. When Colleen used their twin-speak, Sheila knocked her down and made her cry. Marie came to see what happened.

"Work it out among yourselves," she said.

When the girls were on the boat, Sheila pushed her sister again. This time Colleen slipped on the wet deck, and fell backwards with her feet in the air, barely escaping the dangerous ropes.

Sheila was looking at her sister, instead of watching the ropes, and her own foot landed in a moving loop. She couldn't stop what happened next.

Her eyes were locked with Colleen's as she flew over the side. The girls howled in the forbidden language of their birth, and Marie saw what her heart already knew. In an instant the air became an endless scream that gulls amplified as they circled and screeched.

They all knew the first rule of safety: stay in the boat. Never jump in the water for a man overboard. The water was so cold, and current so strong, there would be no way to help if you were in it. Marie couldn't swim, but her leg was already over the side, and Edward had to slap her face to stop her from pulling him into the sea.

As Colleen watched her parents struggle, she collapsed into a small shaking bundle on the deck. Observing her father through a thick fog, as though time itself slowed, she saw him methodically turn the boat around, and set the winch to pull the traps.

Sheila came with the third lobster trap. Her face was lavender, and her feet and legs were twisted in the rope, like stems from a beautiful flower. Her hair glistened in the sun, and her dress puffed up and down with the swells, as graceful as a jellyfish.

They brought her into the boat, and Edward held her up by her feet, slapping her back, hard... again and again... until Marie pushed him aside and sat on the deck cradling the limp child in her arms. She wailed and rocked all the way to the dock. Sheila's open eyes were glassy, like the bait fish that observed everything.

The emergency wagon came to take her to the hospital, but the attendants said they would bring her to Sullivan's Funeral Home instead. The following day a hearse brought Sheila home in a small white coffin.

The O'Learys lived at 45 Elm Street, a cold-water flat on the first floor of a house on The Point, three small bedrooms, a bathroom, a kitchen, and a living room they closed off in winter to conserve fuel.

The undertaker put a wreath on the door, brought the kitchen table into the living room, and covered it with a pale pink cloth. Sheila's coffin was placed on the table. They left the door to the living room open, and a whisper of heat drifted into the cold room with the neighbors who came to look at Sheila.

Their grandfather on their mother's side, "the Don" Petrillo— whose actual name was Anthony—brought two vases of flowers, and placed them at each end of the coffin. When he saw Sheila's body, he started to cry. Then he held Marie's arms very tight and said, "This is what happens when you get knocked up by a shanty Irishman. Italian men don't put their kids in stinking lobster boats and drop them with traps."

Marie's voice cracked. "Colleen accidentally bumped into her. That's why Sheila got caught in the ropes."

Colleen wanted to scream, "That's not what happened!" but she didn't have the words to correct her mother. She couldn't speak when her mother told her to put on her Sunday dress for the funeral, either. Her heart hurt, and she couldn't catch her breath because air didn't go in and out of her easily anymore.

2 Edward and Marie

Edward O'Leary was fourteen years old and in the seventh grade when his mother died. He hadn't paid attention in class because he'd been too busy protecting his older brother Padraig, who was teased mercilessly for his deafness.

He avoided reading because he had to do it slowly, keeping his place on the page with his finger. Since he had not practiced penmanship, Edward printed at a time when everyone else wrote cursive. The result was neat, but it was child-like, and his spelling was lousy. He tried to hide the difficulties he faced, so that people wouldn't laugh at him.

Their farm in Somerset repelled him, and he started to hang around Cap'n O'Connell's boatyard at Steep Brook, in the north end of Fall River. Cap'n, who owned several boats and managed the boatyard, took a liking to him. Young and wiry, Edward didn't look like much, but he was willing to get his hands dirty and took any job he was offered. He worked hard and cheap.

When Cap'n asked why he didn't go to sea instead of working in a dry dock, Edward decided to go to Newport. The first time he wandered down Long Wharf, he found employment as a helper on a lobster boat. The boats were often manned by partners, and if one was sick or injured, the other hired a helper. When one of his bosses allowed him to sleep on the boat, Edward stopped going home. No one came looking for him.

Soon he began to hang around the bars. Pretending he was nursing a beer, he would mention his need for work. He didn't ask where he would be going, how long he'd be gone, or what his duties would be. With a moment's notice he would jump aboard a boat heading toward the horizon. The threat of bad weather didn't concern him.

Fishermen protecting the secrets of their trade were careful around newcomers. But Edward did not miss an opportunity to learn something everywhere he went. Carefully accumulating knowledge from many sources, he painstakingly recorded it in a small notebook he always kept in his shirt pocket.

He learned to set traps with the boat traveling in the direction of the tide, making it less likely that traps would get jumbled up in the surge along the ocean floor. Putting grease in a hollow lead line, he repeatedly dropped it to the bottom. If sand was stuck to the grease when he pulled the line up, he marked the chart "sand" and moved to a different location. Lobsters liked to hide, and traps were most productive on rocky bottoms.

Learning to navigate by dead reckoning, Edward plotted a course from a fixed point like a bell buoy, and used the tachometer to calculate the boat's speed. When the bridge was a mile away, and the engine was going at fifteen hundred revs, he noted how long it took to get from one point to the other, and wrote it in his notebook. He began to ask if he could plot the course from their mooring to the fishing grounds. When he explained that he wanted to practice, many let him try. He consulted the compass, clock, and tachometer constantly. Edward always knew where he was.

Even at the end of his fishing days, when he and everyone else had Loran and radar, he still checked his position by dead reckoning, using methods of navigation as old as Columbus... just in case.

When Edward had his own boat, he left Newport at five a.m. in total darkness and headed toward Block Island twenty-six miles at sea. Two-and-a-half hours later the dawn broke, the fog lifted, and he saw his cork buoy, no bigger than a fire extinguisher, bobbing faithfully nearby, to mark the end of his trawl line. His buoys, identical to the one attached to his wheelhouse, were painted yellow and red, easy colors to see in a slate gray universe. The same colors were identified on his license. It was a foolproof system that made it simple for someone to know from a distance if the buoy attached to a wheelhouse matched the buoys where a man was working.

Edward discovered peace where the land ended, and the rhythm of tide and wind slowed the tempo of his heart. Consoled and complete, he was home. He enjoyed this moment alone with the sea before starting to work. He ate breakfast—a can of sardines with two pieces of bread, and the last dregs of coffee in his thermos.

During clambake season he went back to the farm to see his brother Padraig, and to help their father. He liked ferrying the mill workers across the Taunton River to and from Fall River. But after a few days he couldn't wait to return to Newport.

His first year away from home, Edward found himself idle in the winter. Long Wharf was deserted, the wind howled, and small craft warnings were posted. He was hungry, and needed work. In Providence, he lied about his age and bought a phony birth certificate in order to join the National Maritime Union. A visit to the NMU hall, also in Providence, told him a tanker in port needed a deck hand. Edward signed on as an able-bodied seaman. When he found himself in Galveston, he wandered along the waterfront until a bar reminded him of one in Newport. After a beer, he headed back to his bunk.

Union membership gave him the chance to work at sea while he saved enough money to buy his own boat; and since he didn't have a gambling problem, he managed to keep most of his wages. He met Julius, a shipmate from Newport, who was only a year older than Edward pretended to be, and they became fast friends. Julius was from a large family, and received a lot of mail from his younger sister.

Julius told Edward that when his father went to the hospital to bring his mother and his new brother home, he was told to watch Marie, his little sister. Although he wasn't supposed to touch his father's cigarettes, Julius tried one.

As he began to cough, Marie laughed at him, and ran off with the matches. When she lit a match on her first try, she was so surprised she dropped it on her flannel pajamas. Her chest ignited like a torch, and she ran through the house, screaming. Remembering a Red Cross safety demonstration from school, Julius knocked her down and rolled her in a rug. Doctors at the hospital said it probably saved her life. Burns on her chest and up her neck to her face were severe.

When she came home, a doctor made house calls for months to change her dressings. Terrified, Marie hid when she saw the doctor's car. After they found her, Julius and his aunt, Tanta Bertie, had to hold her down so that the doctor could remove her bandages and debride the scabs that had formed since his last visit. When the ordeal was over, Marie was hysterical and everyone else was spent.

Thick keloid scars covered her chest all the way up her neck, to her chin. Although most people didn't notice because she had a lovely face and always wore dresses with high collars, Marie thought she was ugly. As a consequence, she was very shy, and avoided everyone except her immediate family.

As soon as their ship came back to Providence, Edward and Julius took the bus to Newport together. Posters on telephone poles advertised a circus where they agreed to meet. Edward brought his duffle to the Seaman's Institute on Market Street and arranged for a bed, then went to Long Wharf to see who was around.

A happy noise led him to the end of the road, and Leo's First and Last Stop. Three little people from the circus were inebriated at the bar; it looked like a good time to have a beer and enjoy their antics. Edward heard them promise Stanley, the local little man, a date with a buxom tiny woman, and all the beer he could drink. They wanted him to leave with them and join the show.

Stanley wavered, and the circus workers ordered another pitcher of draft. His specially adapted Harley had caught their attention, and they wanted a ride.

After a while, Edward wandered over to the circus to buy a hotdog. There he ran into Julius, already at a picnic table with his sister Marie and two of their brothers. Marie barely glanced at Edward when they were introduced, but Edward was struck by her beauty. Tongue-tied, he hung around in hope that her brothers would abandon her; he wanted to remain in her presence and didn't know what else to do.

When Julius refused to take her on the Ferris wheel, Edward offered.

Marie said, "No."

But Julius said, "Thanks," and walked away.

Suddenly they were on the Ferris wheel together, and Marie clearly wasn't happy about it. She looked into the distance and didn't say a word. When they jolted to a pause at the top, Edward was as tense as a cat, and he could see by her white knuckles that she was too. Afraid their jumpiness alone would tip the car over, he carefully put his hand on top of hers.

"I'm nervous," he apologized. "You are so pretty."

Looking straight at him for the first time, she smiled and left her hand where it was. They both grinned at their bravery... bravery that had nothing to do with the ride. On their way back to earth, Edward asked her if she would meet him the next day at the Saturday matinee and she agreed. That was the beginning.

When Edward wasn't with Marie, he was thinking about her, and when she didn't know where he was, she was lost, aimless. He frequented her house, but he was so bashful that her brother and father assumed he was there to see Julius. Actually, he hung around Julius because it was the only way he knew to be near Marie.

Finally, she said, "We have to ask my father if we can keep company together."

Edward had no understanding of that, but if she wanted to ask, he was okay with it. On the next Sunday he was invited to their family dinner. When the table was being cleared for dessert, her father asked him to come into the parlor. Mr. Petrillo, a hairy walrus of a man, with a potbelly that protruded like the bow-pulpit on a boat, knew how to intimidate a young man.

Before Edward could sit, Mr. Petrillo said, "What are your intentions?"

Edward had just finished dinner, and his only intention was to have dessert. He was stumped. "What do you mean?"

"I mean are you going to marry my daughter? If not, why are you wasting our time?"

Edward coughed. "I, I don't know."

"What don't you know? Why you're wasting our time? Or if you intend to marry her?"

This was not going well and Edward didn't know what to say. "Ughh."

"How would you support her?"

This last question stunned Edward. Had he said he would marry her? Something had gone wrong and he didn't know how to get back to the place where he was only waiting for dessert.

"Aahh, I don't know."

"Well, you need to figure it out, young man. Julius speaks highly of you; he says you save your money. How much do you have?"

"I'm saving for my own boat."

"I know, I heard about that. You should get a job. Come home at night. Have children. Be there to help your wife. Why don't you check at the mills in Fall River? They need floormen and supervisors. How much have you saved?"

"For my boat. A thousand dollars."

"I know, in the bank. It's good to have a nest egg before you get married."

The money wasn't in the bank. Edward didn't trust the bank, but he didn't want to tell Mr. Petrillo. It was bad enough that he had blurted out the real amount.

Marie came into the room and saved the day with dessert.

"Daddy, Tanta Bertie says please come and have bread pudding while it's warm."

Within a week, Julius went back to the union hall and shipped out, but Edward stayed in Newport. He found a job at O'Connell's Ship Chandlery across the street from Long Wharf and gave up his bed at the Seaman's Institute for a cheap room above a store on Thames Street.

Marie and Edward began to "keep company." Sometimes she came to his room to visit. He knew he should leave town and leave her, because he had no intentions other than the pure enjoyment of being alone with her when they listened to the radio, and comforted each other, and kissed a lot. But he didn't leave.

With the arrival of spring, Edward thought he would die if he didn't get back to sea. Working at the chandlery, he could stand anywhere in the store and watch the boats steaming toward the horizon, all day long. He could almost touch them. When he told Marie it was torture to watch them leave the harbor without him, she became more intent on soothing him; but one morning he didn't dress for his job at the chandlery. He put on his fishing gear and walked to Long Wharf, where a lobsterman hired him for the day.

Serafino Guadagni usually worked alone, but at the moment he was sick with a racking cough, and weak from losing weight. As he spit bright red blood into the water, he explained that he needed help setting his traps before his favorite spots were claimed by others. They had worked together for a week before Serafino was comfortable leaving Edward to work the boat alone, while he went to the doctor.

The next day they were six miles offshore before he said he really didn't know why he was bothering with the traps. The doctor had told him that he had lung cancer.

Serafino rolled a cigarette as he explained his problem to Edward. "I'm going to try to sell the boat, kid. I'll tell the buyer about you, and I hope you can get a job out of it."

"I've got some money saved. How much is the boat?" Edward asked.

"How much do you have?" Serafino wanted to know. "I'd rather sell it to you than anyone else."

Edward didn't like to tell anyone about his savings. He was afraid everyone who found out how much he had, would want that exact amount. "Nine hundred dollars," he lied.

Serafino scratched his head. "I'd like more, but if you're serious, you can give me nine hundred, and I will show you the ropes. I'll help you get started, and be your helper as long as I'm able. You can buy all my gear at half of what it is worth, and pay my family if I die," he paused. "Or you could borrow a hundred dollars, and pay me a thousand for the whole kit and caboodle. Either way, I will help you."

Edward bought the whole kit and caboodle.

He couldn't wait to tell Marie that his dream had come true. The next day he would go to sea driving his own boat, the Gray Gull, with his own helper, Serafino. The boat was small, thirty feet, and beautifully proportioned, perfect for a strong, young man. He imagined himself at the end of a successful day at sea, steaming back to Newport harbor and Marie. In the privacy of his room, she would fold herself around him and rub his tired shoulders while they listened to Sinatra. Pure happiness! Of course, he would be penniless... but who cared?

It turned out that Marie cared. She was not only disappointed, she was horrified. She cried like a hydrant hit by a truck. Her face became blotchy, her nose turned red, and she wouldn't let Edward near her. He didn't know what to do.

Serafino did not become Edward's helper. The day he received the thousand dollars was the last day he worked, and within six weeks he was dead. Edward found it hard to maintain his happiness under the circumstances.

He went to Marie's house, and Mr. Petrillo answered the door.

"Come in, Edward," he said through stiff lips. "Why don't you sit in the parlor with me? I heard about your boat. Congratulations... Why are you here?"

"I came to see Marie."

"Don't you remember our conversation? I advised you to get a proper job. I didn't say a temporary job. I don't want my daughter married to a fisherman who could work all day and catch nothing. Then what would your family eat? No, Edward. I can't allow my daughter to live like that.

"If you planned to get a job and let someone else work the boat, that would be okay. If you planned to make improvements and resell the boat at a higher price than you paid, that would be okay. But to buy a boat and work as a fisherman… that is not okay. Not for my daughter, and not for me."

After the tongue lashing, Edward was more than a little mad, and the mad grew. Old man Petrillo, that horse's backside, would be the death of him. To let off a little steam, Edward went to Leo's First and Last Stop.

With Marie, his life was warm and full of possibility. Without her, it would be the way it had been before they met… cold, empty, hard. Why had he thought it would change? He remembered the way things used to be. When he had no expectations, there were fewer disappointments. Bad luck didn't faze him; they were acquainted.

His friends at the bar were used to the vagaries of life. They took the good with the bad, and had a little fun no matter what. Edward saw the wisdom in that. The bartender at Leo's was as bald as a cue ball, and everyone called him "Skinhead." He was good-humored about it, even when being teased about his mail order "hair restorers" for a scalp as pink and pudgy as a baby's bottom.

Edward listened to Skinhead as he tried to help one of the regular girls. Doris said she needed money to get her car repaired so she could get a job. Rather than spend a fortune on her old jalopy, Skinhead urged her to trade it in for a newer model. He pointed out that a newer vehicle would save future expense and be more reliable. According to him, a woman with a dependable car indicated a woman with good judgment.

Taking her under his wing, he said he admired her common sense. Discussing her situation and limited possibilities made them both thirsty. Skinhead refilled her glass several times before he came up with the idea of raffling her off for the weekend. She was skeptical at first, but he poured another shot into her beer, and Doris agreed.

The raffle poster at the bar drew an amazing response, and tickets sold out quickly; the pot grew to several hundred dollars. On the appointed date, Skinhead picked the winning ticket, and Hervey Flynn won the weekend with Doris. He wore the new flannel shirt he got for Christmas and took Doris to Rocky Point Amusement Park before bringing her back to his mother's house, where he lived. Mrs. Flynn had early dementia, and was very excited that Hervey had finally brought a girl home. She thought Doris was her daughter-in-law.

After the weekend, Doris gave Hervey the raffle money to purchase auto parts wholesale, and he repaired her jalopy on his day off. In the end, Hervey got both Doris and the money, Doris had her old junker purring like a Cadillac, and the bar was buzzing with requests for another raffle.

Within a month, Hervey and Doris got married. And that scared the men something terrible. "That raffle was just a trap!" they said.

For his part, Edward enjoyed all of it... especially after Stanley, the little person, became his best drinking buddy. They drank and talked until their words slurred. Skinhead was Stanley's uncle, and he was allowed to drink "on the cuff" when he didn't have money. He arranged for Edward to have a "cuff account," too... which was helpful on days when lobsters were scarce.

One night, wobbly and belligerent, Stanley revved up his handicap-adapted Harley and attempted to drive it inside the bar. When he was refused entrance, he and Edward stumbled in without the bike, and knocked over a couple of beers while climbing onto the bar shouting, "C'mon, you chickens. Let's have a race!"

Edward hadn't felt so happy since being with Marie. He enjoyed the shouts and laughter and hubbub around him. But he was suddenly "helped" down, told his "on the cuff" account was due, and his business was no longer welcome.

Stanley was sent home, not banished, and Edward was outraged at the unfairness of it. "Blood is thicker than water," someone said to him as he brushed himself off and left. He tried to forget the bad and only remember the fun.

Luckily, The Lobster Claw and The Acorn still wanted his money. Unfortunately, he was more broke than usual, and lobsters were scarce again... and gas was high... and he needed more traps to make more money. There was no choice. To pay his tab, he decided to dig clams and quahogs. It was cold hard work.

To speed things up he concentrated on the quahogs at the end of Wellington Avenue, near King's Park. The water must have been full of nutrients there, because the quahogs were quick-growing, fat, tasty beauties, so thick you could feel them under your waders as you walked. To avoid being spotted in the area near a sign that he supposed said *Private Property*, he dug at night when the moon was full. If he had ever checked during daytime, he would have been surprised to see the sign actually said *Polluted*.

Using recipes he remembered from his father's clambakes, he made chowder and Stuffies (stuffed quahogs). After tasting the delicacies, Skinhead gladly took the seafood in lieu of cash. The items were a hit at the bar, and Edward was praised for his culinary talent... a skill he intended to use to pay his tab in the future.

A few days later, Marie was standing on the dock waiting for Edward and the Gray Gull to return to Long Wharf. His heart rejoiced at the sight of her. Then, without a hug, or even the smallest bit of small talk, she told him she thought she was pregnant. He turned away. It was awful the way people sprang the bad news of their expectations on him.

Pregnant! The word hit him like a bat, a bat wielded by an arrogant old creep named Petrillo. Edward had never been invited to use the nitwit's first name. Maybe he didn't have a name. His own sister, Tanta Bertie, called him "The Mista."

Edward's eyes went from his feet to the horizon. He wished a trap door would spring open, dropping him into a tunnel that sucked him to China and spit him out. He wanted to be safely away from this mess, leaving only a ripple and a *whooshing* sound behind.

"Does your father know?" he asked her.

"Not yet, but my aunt suspects."

Marie's mother had died in childbirth and her father's sister, Tanta Bertie, was an old maid with a hairy wart on her upper lip, who came from Italy to raise the Petrillo children. In return she had a roof over her head and a small room near the kitchen, not to mention indoor plumbing and electricity. Mr. Petrillo called her a saint, but she reminded Edward of a witch in a Grimm's fairy tale. You might not think she was nearby, but she was always near a door or a curtain, peeking out to see if an immigration official had come to take her. She didn't miss a thing, and her soft felt slippers made no noise, perfect for sneakiness.

"I wrote a letter to Julius, asking him what to do," Marie continued.

"What did he s-s-say?" Edward stuttered.

Marie answered, "I couldn't bring myself to mail the letter. Besides, he comes home on Friday."

Edward expected Julius to kill him on Friday. But Julius was so mired in his own problems, he did not notice the lack of mail from Marie.

Mr. Petrillo expected Julius to bring a nice Italian-Catholic girl home to meet him some day, but Julius wanted to marry Winifred Wysockie. Not only was she a Polish-Catholic, but she lived in Newark, New Jersey, and wouldn't consider a move to Newport, Rhode Island.

"The Mista" refused to meet her on the grounds of "religious principles" because, according to him, Italian-Catholics were not allowed to date, never mind marry Polish-Catholics.

Forced to reconsider their plans, the couple decided to elope, get an apartment in Newark, and avoid contact with the Petrillo family until after the baby was born. When Julius told Marie about this, he omitted the part about the baby.

He said, "We want you and Edward to come with us, and be our witnesses at the Justice of the Peace."

Her eyes swimming, Marie listened quietly before telling her brother that Edward had quit his job and bought a boat. Julius somberly held her shoulders and stared straight into her soul.

"Look, Marie," he said. "You can't ask Edward to give up the sea, and you need to stop acting like our dad is God Almighty. You don't want to end up like Tanta Bertie, do you?"

"What do you mean?"

"Would you change places with her? She lives in her brother's house, takes care of her brother's children, and everyone else's life is more important than her own. If you don't take charge of your life, you may end up like Tanta Bertie... an old hag without a family of your own, cooking and cleaning up after other people until you drop dead."

The next day, Marie met Edward at the dock again. She told him that Julius and Winifred were going to elope, and had asked them to come along to New York and act as witnesses.

Edward liked the idea of a trip with Marie, and readily agreed.

"Do you want to get married when they do?" Marie asked. "They could stand up for us, after we stood up for them."

"I have no money," Edward said.

"Neither have I," answered Marie. "But I love you."

"Okay," he said.

That weekend Marie and Edward, and Julius and Winnie, eloped. At the end of a very long day, and a quick ceremony at a Justice of the Peace, they checked into a small motel for their honeymoon. When Winnie told Julius that she had seen Marie throw up in the bathroom, and she thought that his sister was pregnant too, he became furious. He accused Winnie of bad-mouthing an innocent Marie, who was only carsick because she had been riding all day long to accommodate their hasty wedding.

As a result of the argument that followed, Winnie and Julius stopped speaking to each other and went to bed mad. The next morning, they were still not speaking.

Julius almost fainted when Marie announced her pregnancy over coffee. Then Winnie followed with her own disclosure, and both couples ordered a huge breakfast to celebrate.

As soon as Marie and Edward returned to Newport, they found a small apartment and settled into a life that made Edward happier than he had ever been. Marie took a sewing job in a second-floor sweat-shop on Thames Street, while Edward worked on the Gray Gull.

Mr. Petrillo pretended Marie and her brother didn't exist. Neither couple missed him or his overbearing ways. The birth of the twins softened his heart enough to come to the hospital to see his daughter Marie with her babies Colleen and Sheila, his first grandchildren. But he avoided Edward. Nothing could change his opinion that his daughter was too good to be married to a lobsterman.

Sometimes Edward stopped to have a beer on his way home. He was overwhelmed with the way two tiny babies took over the whole apartment with diapers, and knitted hats, and small flannel sleeping bags. It was next to impossible for him to get to sleep with their constant mewling and Marie jumping out of bed to tend them. There wasn't a moment's peace to be had. He was exhausted and thwarted.

Staying home with Sheila and Colleen until they were old enough to be left at a nursery meant Marie now sewed "piece-work" at home, and barely made any money. They were almost completely dependent on Edward's ability to earn a living. Results were erratic, and the stress caused by the uncertainty of his occupation led Edward to stop in the bars more frequently. A few drinks settled him down, rounded out the jagged corners of the day, and brought him a little cheer.

If Marie had known about the bar activities that helped raise his spirits, she would have ridiculed them. She had no appreciation for a man's hard work, or the kind of fun he needed. She was a wet blanket, and Edward tried to make sure she didn't know much about his friends at Leo's First and Last Stop, The Acorn, and The Lobster Claw.

He dreamed of becoming a crooner like Sinatra or Como. After the correct amount of alcohol, he closed his eyes and rocked back on his heels to perform. Occasionally he was so moved by his own vocal gift that unbidden tears streamed down his cheeks. People familiar with his talent bought him a beer and requested "Danny Boy" or "Too Ra Loo Ra Loo Ra."

Occasionally, he used the pay phone to call Charity, his half-sister in New York (person to person collect). Charity knew enough to refuse the charges. The phone call was his signal that he was thinking of her. Once Edward managed to sing "Happy Birthday" as the operator pulled the plug. Another time, all the people around him joined in the singing. Charity must have loved it.

Although he tried to perform at home, he wasn't appreciated by his family.

Marie would go nuts if he tried to venture upstairs to the DiPhillipos' apartment to ask to use their phone. And the DiPhillipos were too backward to know the trick of making a collect call to someone who refused the charges on purpose. When he tried to explain, they looked at him as though he was nuts.

Charity knew what to do; she was the one who taught Edward how rich people called long distance without paying. But Marie took the fun out of Edward singing a song to his sister. She spoiled the whole idea; marriage to Marie was a burden.

Edward's voice wasn't great, but he thought he would sound as good as Perry Como if he had music in the background. And if he learned to cut hair and got a job in a barbershop, he might have a good chance of being discovered. After all, lots of famous people came to Newport.

The previous summer Bing Crosby's picture had been on the front page of the *Newport Daily News,* standing in front of a mansion on Ocean Drive, holding his hat in a thirty-knot wind. One of the men at The Acorn said he was there to take those pictures, and as soon as Bing moved his hand, the hat blew away with his hair inside it. The men in the bar were stunned. "Bing wears a rug!" they shouted.

After hearing him talk about Bing, Perry, and the good fortune of the barber who became a singing star, someone brought a pair of hair clippers to Leo's and left them for Edward.

"Give it a shot, kid," was Skinhead's advice as he handed him the bag.

Edward was anxious to learn how to cut hair, so that he could be discovered quickly and start singing on the radio. If he had a son, he could practice with the clippers, but lacking a boy didn't stop him. He went across the street to where Walter, a neighbor child about three or four years old, was playing, and offered the boy a nickel for candy. Walter soon sat on Edward's kitchen table holding the nickel while the lobsterman warmed up the clippers. They were hard to handle and tended to jump around, leaving Walter's head spotted with pink, bald places. The more Edward tried to even out the patches, the worse they became. The kid looked like a dog with the mange.

When his whining and fidgeting made further corrections impossible, Edward gave Walter a dime instead of a nickel, and covered his wounds with Vaseline, before putting a baseball hat on him and sending him back outside to play. Walter's mother blew the whole thing out of proportion, and Marie went berserk.

Unable to get any hair-cutting experience, Edward returned the clippers and stopped singing. There was no longer a reason to learn the barbering trade; he would never be discovered, or become a singing sensation.

If he had a boat, he fished. If he didn't have a boat, he went to the union hall and shipped out. At sea, he worked; on shore, he drank. When the money for drinking was gone, he went back to sea and earned the money to come ashore; then he drank until he ran out of money, and the cycle began anew.

There was nothing in Edward's future. His dream was dead like the rest of his life. Rent and groceries, and electricity, and rope, and fishing licenses, and mooring fees. and material to make dresses, and yarn to make sweaters, and who knows what else, sucked his pockets dry. Some people were born rich; some, like Como and Sinatra, just opened their mouths and became rich. Edward couldn't win because the deck was stacked against the ordinary stiff. He had learned that the hard way.

Skinhead said that if you get enough money to buy a house, the government will keep track of the improvements you make to it, and raise your taxes. Taxes made no sense to Edward. Why try to improve your standard of living if the government was going to penalize you for it? If making more meant keeping less, what chance did a little guy have? It was better to stay under the level of the tax system altogether. Edward was an expert.

3 Marie and Edward

Marie, the only one of ten children to graduate high school, hoped to get a good government job in the school lunch program. It would provide a steady paycheck, a schedule that was the same as her twins' school, and eventually a small retirement. Government jobs were hard to come by, and people waited years for an opening. Meanwhile, Marie worked as a seamstress, or a waitress at the Officer's Club on the Naval Base.

At the Officer's Club, Marie learned the proper way to set a table, and she made sure to teach her children. The girls learned that utensils were placed alongside the plate in the order which they were to be used, by the hand that uses them. The furthest from the plate was to be used first. Knives were always on the right, with the cutting blade toward the plate, and forks were always to the left of the plate (the oyster fork being the only exception... which is placed on the right if it is being used).

Before dinner Marie opened the *Daily News* and spread it on the table. The plates and utensils were put in their correct places, and at the end of dinner the newspaper was folded up and thrown away. Colleen and Sheila loved having the newspaper on the table, because their mother put the comics between them, and helped them with the pictures and the words. That's how they learned to read. When they were big enough to walk that far, Marie took them to the library once a week. It was a long trek, but it was a delight to be left in the children's room of Newport Library to pick out as many books as they could carry home.

All fun ended when Sheila died. Edward's drinking increased, and the boat had a motor problem he couldn't afford to fix; even the weather turned against him.

With the boat laid up, he couldn't get offshore to save his gear, and a Nor'easter smashed his traps to smithereens against underwater rocks. Marie wrung her hands and prayed. Her husband was back at the beginning with no money to buy gear, build traps, or repair the motor.

Luckily, Skinhead knew someone who managed to get the motor started with a temporary fix. Edward packed a duffle and chugged up to O'Leary's Point where his brother Padraig still lived on what was left of the old farm at the end of O'Leary Road. Edward tied up to a mooring near shore and walked up the lane past the simple cottage he once called home. As usual, his brother was in the barn. They had a few beers and Padraig agreed to take care of the boat. He drove Edward to the union hall in Providence, where he shipped out on a tanker.

Four months later he came back with some money. By then Marie had been alone and broke for so long that she was glad to see him. They sent Colleen to Ruthie's store to buy a bag of penny candy and disappeared into the bedroom for a nap. Marie was always tired, and coming home made Edward tired too. Their naps brought back sharp memories of Sheila; the music of her laughter was still fresh. But the laughter disappeared faster than the candy, and everyone's pleasure was short lived. A few weeks after his return, while he still had the money for repairs, Edward went to Somerset to get the boat fixed. It was time to go lobstering again.

When he came to the end of the lane after the bus ride from Newport and a long walk, he didn't see his boat at its mooring. His stomach instantly became queasy and uncomfortable, squeezed as tight as a fist. Edward walked back to the barn, looking for Padraig, his mind full of possibilities that explained the absence of both the boat and his brother. Maybe the engine had been repaired, and Padraig had taken it for a test-ride. Maybe he had set a few traps and was pulling them up to get dinner. Maybe.

Edward waited with a gut full of dread. Finally, Padraig drove up in a delivery truck, overjoyed to see him. He explained in gestures and grunts that Edward's friends had come to repair the motor and take the boat back to him in Newport.

Padraig didn't know the friends' names, but he had seen them on the boat, and he went out on a skiff to talk to them. They assured him they were working on the motor at Edward's request. They even borrowed a few tools from the barn and returned them before they left with the boat.

Edward marched back and forth, threw rocks, and asked the same question again and again. "Who were they?" What made Padraig believe he had a friend? Edward cursed and shouted. He kicked the ground and raised his hand to hit his brother. But there was no hope for it. He had been back for more than a week, resting a little, wetting his whistle. He had spoken of his boat, the repair it needed, the location of its mooring, and the fact that he was taking a little time off. He might have said that his brother was as dumb as a whale-turd, for all he knew.

Now the boat was gone, and he needed a drink.

Padraig was in a state. There was no dealing with his whirlwind of gestures and sounds and exclamations. He punched the air and the truck, threw his hat on the ground, and picked it up only to throw it down again. Taking half a fat cigar from his pocket, he chomped the end of it to mush, in between emphatic spits. Edward had never seen him so upset. Finally, they calmed down enough to go for beer, a lot of beer. With the beer, and some moonshine from the barn, they managed to drown their fury.

The next day, Edward took the bus back to Newport and went straight to Leo's First and Last Stop to tell Skinhead about the boat burglary. He didn't want to go home because he knew that when Marie found out the boat was gone, she would immediately want the money he had set aside to repair the motor. That's all she thought about, money!

From Leo's he went to The Acorn and The Lobster Claw. It was two drunken days before someone asked, "What did the police and the harbor-master say?"

The question sobered Edward up so much that he went to the police station to report the burglary. Captain DiVito took notes, and picked up the phone to call the harbormaster, while Edward sat fiddling with his hat brim.

"What did they say when you reported this in Somerset?" (where the boat was actually stolen) he asked, "Or Fall River?" (which was in spitting distance, and being larger, had a harbor master).

Edward looked stricken. "I'm on my way to do that now," he replied quietly.

Captain DiVito sighed, put the phone down, and took his glasses off.

"All this time," he said. "The Gray Gull is probably in an out-of-the-way harbor with a new name, a new paint job, and a new owner! I will check, but we are probably too late to catch them."

Edward looked lost.

"What are you going to do without a boat?" DiVito asked.

"I don't know," Edward answered.

"You're young, why don't you join the Navy? During the war they made warrant officers out of young guys who knew the harbor like you do."

"Maybe," Edward said as he left.

Captain DiVito looked at his patrolman. "You know that guy?"

"I seen him in his cups singing Irish songs at Leo's First and Last Stop," the cop replied.

"Me too. Seems like a dipshit," DiVito responded.

Later, at Leo's, Edward mentioned that joining the Navy seemed like a good way to have a life at sea without having to own a boat.

Skinhead brought him a draft. "The Navy is nothing but logs and reports," he said. "They do more paperwork than the newspapers."

That was enough for Edward. Eventually he told Marie, who told everyone else, he had been asked to join the Navy, but he couldn't put up with the logs and reports. Edward stayed away from paperwork.

The boat was gone. He had spent all his money, he felt awful, and he was sober. Things were so bad there was nothing to do but go home with the bad news that he was behind the eight ball again. Sitting and rocking in his chair for days, he wore the terrycloth bathrobe Marie had made for him last Christmas. There was no point in getting dressed.

Marie watched him and prayed about him, and got sick with migraines, and ulcers, and arthritis, while Edward spiked his coffee with whiskey from little bottles he hid around the apartment. Marie was tired of working for money her husband spent before she could take care of essentials. Every time she found his little bottles of liquor, she poured some of it on the fruitcakes she made. Then she added water to the little bottle and put it back where she found it. She knew they were never going to be prepared for storms in the future because they hadn't finished paying for the ones in the past.

Like a broken record, Marie said she didn't want Edward around unless he quit drinking. Colleen witnessed her father's debasement with eyes full of disappointment, mute in the blizzard of cruel words. Edward sometimes thought he saw Sheila in her matching dress, standing beside Colleen. He didn't know which was worse, the loss of his daughter, his thirst for alcohol, or the need for a boat.

He didn't own a boat anymore, and he didn't know how he'd ever get one again. But drinking was different. He knew he could quit. Once he gave it up for a week. But, now, the days had sharp edges. Weather reports and foghorns mocked him. When he could no longer get a drink on the cuff, he shipped out.

When he came back with a few bucks, he drank until the money was gone, and he was forced to dig clams. Then he shipped out again. Bad luck followed him like a stray dog after a meat truck, while he sat home by the radio and rocked, and ruminated, and smoked, and wondered how the good days had turned into these days.

There was a man in Newport who drove the drycleaner's truck. His daughter had been run over by the train while she was playing on the railroad tracks. Afterwards, her father always wore sunglasses. Following Sheila's death, Edward learned why. His own eyes frightened him; surely they would scare other people. When he shaved, his pupils expanded, beckoning him to enter their transparent road to hell. He found a pair of sunglasses, and wore them to protect the general public.

Edward felt as though gravity did not keep him properly attached to the earth. Staring into his failures, he concentrated on becoming heavy enough to attach himself to something. A shot of whiskey dropped into a beer sometimes made him heavier than plain draft. Thinking about it all the time was exhausting, but it helped him to get to the place where his eyelids were heavy enough to close, and he could sleep.

While he was asleep, the past became the present and he was able to slip through to the other side as easily as a drop of rain joins a puddle. Edward's ability to exist without his body was wonderful, but temporary. When he woke, he was back in the present, and Sheila was dead. He hurt all over, and his gravity levels were so dangerously low, he was afraid a strong gust of wind would knock him off his feet.

Later, when they had a car, he recognized the same sensation as he drove toward the horizon on a straight flat road. In the distance he could see a place where the air was wavy and shimmery, like millions of strips of aluminum foil hanging at the edge of the universe and reflecting light. The place retreated as he approached, but he knew that if he could get there, he would drive right through the moment where turbulence and chaos meet. The rules of physics would bend, and the atmosphere on the other side would change his perception of reality.

With the abandonment of rules of time and matter, Edward thought the past and the present could coexist, and he would be with Sheila. Sometimes his need was so critical it vibrated in the air around him. His eyes ached from darting constantly to catch sight of her as she stepped around a corner or disappeared under someone's umbrella. He recognized the color of her hair, or her jacket. Sometimes she was in a store window, or just leaving it.

If he was in a crowd crossing a street and looked at his feet, he occasionally saw her shoe at the edge of his peripheral vision. Sometimes his eyes, hungry for Sheila, made a mistake, and it was only Colleen that he saw. Then his skin itched with discomfort and fresh air smelled like vinegar. Breathing made him sick to his stomach, and even though he was starved and his gut churned, he couldn't eat. Not that it mattered.

He stayed away from home because Marie's long faces and heaving sighs made him miserable. Moreover, Colleen's inability to speak reminded him of his pathetic deaf brother. Colleen didn't smile at him and flirt with him for penny candy. She didn't dance on his feet when "Mexicali Rose" played on the radio. She didn't steal a sip of coffee from his cup when he pretended not to look, and she never touched his shoulder when she passed his chair. Sheila had been attached like a barnacle to his heart, his brain, and his gut, and although Colleen was her spitting image, she lacked whatever it was that made Sheila, Sheila.

At home he turned himself inside out to hide his need. His social life used to be separate from his home life, but suddenly all he had was home. He put cough medicine, or vanilla extract, or whatever contained alcohol, in his coffee cup. But there was never enough, and he couldn't rest until there wasn't a drop of alcohol in the house.

Edward had never wanted to be a husband or a father. There were so many things he had wanted in life that didn't happen... good things that would never happen now that this family, that he didn't want to begin with, had somehow taken over every single minute of his existence. At first, he liked Marie, wanted to be loved by her, and worried over by her. Even when she was mad at him, she was paying attention, and he liked it... in the beginning. But it had been a long time since the beginning, and he didn't like any part of the present.

It was a happy day for Marie when she started to work in the school lunch program. Like the other workers, she carried an oversized, black-plastic purse to transport leftovers home. The program, which used government surplus to provide staples, delivered sawed-in-half frozen turkeys to schools for the holidays. Marie managed to wrestle one into her plastic mini-suitcase acting as a pocket book.

"Christmas dinner in the purse?" Edward asked, as he watched his wife hauling the awkward handbag through the door. His joke fell flat; they were all off-kilter as they faced another Christmas without Sheila. Colleen knew from sad experience that Edward was sure to ruin the holiday.

This time, on Christmas Eve, wearing her first new hat in years, Marie tried to shame him into attending midnight mass. Expecting his usual refusal, she said, "Come on, Colleen. We will pray for his lost soul."

Suddenly, he erupted in a tirade which didn't end until he had followed them out the front door. There, in the presence of neighbors also leaving for church, Marie stood slack-jawed while Edward, tipsy from a long day on the sauce, bellowed, "And I wouldn't go anywhere with a woman wearing a red hat like a floozy."

Tears flowed in narrow lines down Marie's powdered cheeks as she straightened her shoulders in her threadbare coat, and turned to Colleen. "Do you like my hat?"

Colleen nodded without raising her eyes to the flaming feathers. Her inability to meet Marie's gaze resulted in fresh tears, and by the time they reached church, her mother's face had a melted look. All the seats were taken, and they were mashed together in the crowded back, rocking on their feet, overpowered by the smell of damp wool and Old Spice aftershave.

Colleen remembered their last Christmas with Sheila, when they were a family with seats. She and Sheila had started to giggle when the priest let out a fart as loud as a truck backfire, and the soprano screeched off-key while singing "O Holy Night." Once started, they couldn't stop. They muffled their unholy laughter in scarves, but just when one regained composure, the other lost it. They pretended to cough, then started laughing again.

But they stopped laughing when they came home to find the house looking like the aftermath of a disaster. Edward must have hidden some drinking money and forgotten where he put it, because every drawer was open, every rug askew, every picture had been taken off the wall, and his majesty himself was snoring on the couch. He must have found some of his small liquor bottles. Marie took her red hat off and put it on top of the trash.

Edward used to say Marie was "so naive that people took advantage of her, and if he didn't take money from her purse, she would waste it, or lose it." He only hid it under a rug, or behind a picture on the wall, or folded up in the sock he was wearing, to make sure it would be there in an emergency, if they needed it to buy cough medicine or something. Otherwise, Marie would "spend every dime they had."

Most ridiculous of all, Marie actually wanted to get a checking account and put her whole paycheck in the bank... "as if the bank wouldn't take full advantage of that!" He didn't know where she got the idea that they needed a bank to pay their bills. How could someone as trusting as she was survive in this dog-eat-dog world?

Banks needed to be carefully watched. They were in a position to take your money, and they did so at every opportunity. Taking a little at a time, some from one account, and some from another, a dollar here and a dollar there, it added up. If they were caught, they would say there had been a mistake. People couldn't spend all their time watching the bank; Edward was wise to their pilfering.

At home, bad memories hung on a nail with his bathrobe, bubbled up from the sink, looked through dark windows when he turned on a light, and tied him to his chair with rope while he dozed. Marie and Colleen were not pleased by his company. From time to time, he shipped out without saying goodbye, and sometimes he didn't send money home. Edward rarely wrote even a postcard; between ships he spent more and more time in the bars.

At The Lobster Claw he met a woman named Brenda who also liked to drink. Her husband was a sailor who had been washed off the deck of a Navy ship in heavy seas. Since they hadn't recovered his body, she didn't need a burial, and that saved money. Some of her money came from having her husband die while on active duty, and some came from death benefits. In any case, Edward and Brenda had a lot in common. She talked about Roger, and he cried about Sheila.

Initially, Marie thought Edward had gone to the union hall and had to leave immediately. She worked days and worried nights, thinking that, as usual, he would get a message to her. When no message came, she was afraid he was gone forever. After a week had passed, she went upstairs to borrow the DiPhillipos' phone.

First she called Leo's, and then The Acorn, and finally, The Lobster Claw. When she asked for Edward, she heard his voice in the background. "Tell her O'Leary left a while ago." One of their neighbors gasped on the party line, and Marie dropped the phone. She and Colleen cried.

Seeing her mother upset bothered Colleen tremendously and she walked around exhausted, as though she had been up all night. It wasn't until she dreamed that Sheila came through the window to comfort her, that she had peace, as soothing as a lullaby.

One day Colleen decided to play with the kids on Bridge Street and she noticed her father coming out of The Lobster Claw with a lady. He wobbled a few blocks down Second Street to the entrance for the apartment above Ruthie's Store. Breathless and scared, Colleen hurried home to tell her mother.

Marie was so furious she rushed down the street still wearing her school lunch uniform. Colleen was aghast; her mother hadn't even put on a coat or changed her work shoes. Marie rushed the few blocks to the home-wrecker's apartment and instead of ringing the bell, she entered the vestibule and rushed up the stairs to the inside front door.

Bursting in without knocking, she saw a tranquil scene. Her husband was sitting on the couch while a small boy sat on the floor playing with his hat. No one had ever been allowed to touch Edward's hat... not even Sheila when she was alive.

The woman, whose name she would learn was Brenda, stood at the kitchen table making a peanut butter sandwich. Edward was dumbfounded by his wife's arrival. Marie had swirled into the room like a gale force wind, and grabbed his hat from the child's hands. She threw it on the floor and stomped on it. Then she took his cup of coffee from the table and poured it on top of the hat.

Edward said, "Now Marie, go home. Go home, Marie. You don't belong here."

He was right. She didn't belong there any more than he did. The kid was screaming, a woman was yelling, and Marie's no-good husband was sending *her* away.

"Give me your key and give me your money," she yelled.

Reaching into his pocket, Edward pulled out his key to their apartment, and showed her the two dollars that he had left.

Marie took both. "Take off your shoes," she said.

"Marie, you're crazy. Stop making a fool of yourself and go home," Edward said. He still couldn't believe the nerve of her.

"Take off your shoes," she repeated and bent down to pull the laces.

He could see this wouldn't end until he was barefoot.

Colleen had arrived in tears and was attempting to pull her mother toward the door. Edward would have sworn it was Sheila in her plaid dress. It scared him.

The kid was still crying and Brenda was screaming, "Get out of my house! You're all crazy. I'm calling the police!"

Edward, who had recently had a problem with the police, calmly said, "Brenda, this is Marie. Don't call the police. She's going to leave now."

While he was speaking, Marie pulled ten dollars out of his sock, then she turned and left. When she got home, she put all of Edward's belongings in two brown paper bags and left them on the sidewalk. She and Colleen cried together.

Boiling mad, Marie was afraid she would not be able to raise Colleen alone. Colleen was mortified that the whole nightmare had taken place in full view of anyone with normal vision. Being related to these people was a cruel fate.

None of this would have happened if Sheila was alive. Her father wouldn't be drunk, he wouldn't have a new woman, and no strange kid would be playing with his hat. Her mother wouldn't be hysterical and out of control in the street. She would be able to speak and breathe and endure her life.

Sheila had been part of every breath Colleen took. Before she could speak, Sheila had known her thoughts and feelings. Colleen didn't know how to describe the half-a-life she had left... the worst possible half.

She cried herself to sleep that night, and Sheila came in a dream to comfort her, lifting her spirit like a soaring bird on a strong current of wind.

4 Uncle Nick and Colleen

Colleen, who hadn't spoken since her sister's funeral, was stunned when her mother told her that Uncle Nick, the tailor, wanted her to model one of the fancy, first-communion dresses he imported from Italy. She could pick the dress and keep it after they took pictures for advertising.

The ad in the Newport Daily News said, "*Beautiful handmade dresses... available, including alterations, for prices as reasonable as factory-produced.*"

Marie and Colleen were elated.

When Marie told Uncle Nick she had started to work a second job, as a waitress in her cousin Vito's Italian restaurant during the dinner hours, he said, "Timing is everything." And he offered to watch Colleen on the days Marie worked in the restaurant.

Thereafter, Colleen walked eight blocks to the tailor shop and waited for her mother, while Nick caught up on his alterations.

Uncle Nick spoiled her. His hand followed a chain into his pocket and pulled out his watch. "Candy time," he smiled. His drawer was so full of sweets it looked like Halloween. He told her the candy had to remain their secret.

According to the doctor, Colleen was physically able to speak... a voluntary mute. He said she would probably talk again when she recovered from the trauma of watching her twin die. Colleen was almost bursting with words, but her mother took comfort in her silence. Nick found it calming as well. He said women should pay attention to their appearance and try to be beautiful. At the shop, Colleen learned a lot about clothes.

"It is amazing how people are used to junk, with patterns and stripes that don't match at the seams. Quality of fabric and correct fit are the foundation of self-confidence. When clothes fit, they make you feel good," he declared.

He made Colleen fussy, according to Marie. Actually, he instructed her in a lot of things. Sometimes he took pictures of her with his camera for advertising. He held her on his lap and read her homework to her, while he rubbed her back and sounded out the hard words, without ever trying to get her to say them. Everyone pressured her to speak, but not Uncle Nick.

Colleen would always remember him taking off his thimble before she felt his hand warm on her thigh, on top of her school clothes, while he rubbed her stomach to see if it was full of chocolate.

They ate a lot of candy. Sometimes they had a little hot cocoa and they napped on the overstuffed chaise in the back. His breathing was soft and even, like Sheila's, in time with her own. At home she was disturbed by noises like radio static when she tried to fall asleep. But it was easy to sleep at the shop, at first.

Marie was worried sick about how she was going to pay the rent and the tab at Ruthie's store and the electric and oil bill. Colleen worried too. Sometimes on the way home from the tailor shop, they went into the alley behind the drug store to buy pills from the pharmacist, Doctor Bob. Marie told Colleen that although some people didn't believe he was as good as the doctor, she did.

Without the pills that gave her enough energy for two jobs, she just couldn't keep going; and if the medicine was real, she supposed the doctor was too. When her mother came to pick her up at the tailor shop, she often turned to Uncle Nick and said, "I'm lucky that I have you. You are the only one who is there for me when I really need it."

"Timing is everything, sweetie," he would say with a smile.

Edward lived with Brenda a few blocks away from his family. His financial help was sporadic, and he made no attempt to see Colleen.

Marie made excuses for everything he did and didn't do: it was the fault of the bars that allowed him to drink on the cuff, and it was Brenda's fault for taking him in. It was his father's fault for being a bad role model, his mother's fault for dying young, his brother's fault for being a burden, his teacher's fault for letting him quit school, and at the bottom of it all, it was the death of his baby girl that killed the man he could be, if only he didn't drink.

Colleen didn't care; she liked the peace in their small apartment when Marie had her pills. One day she wrote her mother a note saying she could take care of herself, and didn't need Uncle Nick to babysit anymore.

Marie disagreed. "How can I leave you alone?" she asked. "If something happened, how would anyone know? After you start speaking again, you can be your own babysitter."

Colleen had a terrible toothache. Her mother put a poultice in her cheek and gave her an aspirin. That afternoon, even though she was hungry, the throbbing was so intense she refused Uncle Nick's candy. The poultice did not work, and her jaw was swollen.

Marie took her to the free dental clinic in the basement of city hall. The dentist looked into Colleen's mouth and said, "That tooth needs to come out." He turned to get his pliers, as tears streamed down Colleen's cheeks.

"This will be over in a second and you will feel much better," he declared. "Open wide."

He reached into her mouth and yanked the tooth. It rocked on its roots, but stayed put.

"Stubborn bugger," he complained.

He pulled the tooth again, harder. This time it came out and he pressed a gauze pad in her bloody mouth.

"Have her rinse with warm salt water and give her an aspirin," he said over Colleen's sobs.

Marie was furious. "You didn't even give her a shot," she said.

"That was a baby tooth and this is the free dental clinic. We save shots for serious problems," he replied.

Marie took Colleen's hand and left muttering, "Sadist," loud enough for the dentist to hear.

The next day, still swollen and sore, her mother took Colleen to her Aunt Janet's for a haircut, to cheer her up. Janet offered them a piece of fancy candy.

"Did Uncle Nick bring this to you?" Marie asked.

"Yes. Every time he comes here, he brings me a box of fancy chocolates from his importer."

Marie said, "He takes care of Colleen for a few hours while I work the dinner shift at Uncle Vito's. It has been a big help."

"What will you do in September?" Aunt Janet wondered.

Marie and Colleen looked up. "What are you talking about?"

"I'm sorry. I shouldn't have said anything. Nick was here yesterday and I thought he said he would be taking care of Lucia instead of Colleen. I must have misunderstood." Janet put a towel around Colleen's shoulders and started to comb her bangs straight down in front of her eyes.

"I eat too much candy," the child said.

Her mother and Janet looked at each other. They were so unused to hearing Colleen's voice they didn't recognize it.

Marie spoke up, "No... you don't eat candy. I never buy candy."

She wanted to scream with joy, but was afraid that if she called attention to the words, they would stop. Janet's eyes were huge when they met Marie's gaze.

Marie's hand covered her astonished heart. "And that Torrone costs a fortune... if you can find it," she added.

"But I ate a lot of it, and I drank too much hot cocoa. And my tooth rotted."

Her mother and Janet hugged her between them.

Marie said, "Thank God, you are speaking, Colleen. But it takes a long time to get a cavity like yours. A few candies and hot cocoas cannot do that."

"It was a long time, and it wasn't a few candies," Colleen remarked.

Janet looked at Marie. "Nick makes himself a creme de cacao sometimes," she said.

"That's alcoholic!" Marie replied. "Surely you are not suggesting."

"No. I'm not suggesting."

They looked at each other again.

"What do you do after you have the hot cocoa?" Marie asked.

"We go to sleep," Colleen said.

The scissors stopped.

"Is it okay if I call Veronica to see if Nick is really going to take care of Lucia?" Marie asked as she stepped into the other room.

Janet turned the radio on. "Sure. And let's have a little music."

When Marie came back, she was ashen.

"Did I misunderstand?" Janet asked.

"No. Shhh," Marie answered as she pointed to Colleen, and put her finger to her lips.

Janet spritzed Colleen's bangs and put her under the dryer. "You need five minutes to set," she said, as she handed Colleen a movie magazine, and turned to face Marie.

"What?" Janet asked.

"Veronica's sister Anna had a fit when she heard that Nick was going to watch Lucia. Anna says no one believed her when she was molested by Nick as a child. Then one of the old aunts told Veronica there had been rumors about him for years. They thought he was too old to be a problem anymore."

"What are you going to do?" Janet asked.

"I'm going to get Veronica and Anna to go with me to talk to Grandfather Don," Marie said.

Janet turned the dryer off and combed Colleen's bangs again.

"He doesn't do anything bad," Colleen said with agitation. "He's very nice. He rubs my back, he holds me on his lap and reads to me, we drink cocoa, we take a nap."

Her mother told her to calm down. "I didn't say anything was bad. But you are not going to stay at the shop again, and Lucia isn't going to be staying there either. I'm too tired to work two jobs anymore, and that is all there is to it." Marie was adamant.

When the women met with Grandfather Don, he kept his lawyer in the office with them. "This is serious," he said. "Nick has abused your trust, and the trust of our family. He will be held accountable. I will look into this and tell you what I find."

A week later they met with Grandfather Don again. He told them that the importer had been getting film developed for Nick in Europe. The pictures were of a child. In most of the pictures the child appeared to be asleep.

Marie and Janet spoke in unison, "Should we go to the police?"

"Definitely not," Grandfather said. "The importer is my friend too. Let me get the negatives, and fix this quietly. We need to protect our children. We don't want to see them in the daily news."

They thanked him and left.

Grandfather Don called his nephew in Providence. "Lorenzo, I need to ask a favor," he said. "I have a cancer here and I need a talented surgeon who is available to operate immediately, before it spreads. And the surgeon will be saving a child. If the specialist has a daughter, tell him to bring me a picture of her."

Within twenty-four hours Grandfather Don was showing pictures of Colleen to Mario, the specialist from Providence. "I understand this little girl is the age of your daughter," he said.

"Yes, Godfather," was Mario's reply.

"Did you bring a picture?"

"Yes, Godfather," he said and handed over a picture of his daughter in her first communion dress.

"Beautiful girl. Bring it with these other pictures, and show them to Nick. Because, under our noses, for many years, this cockroach has been disrespecting his family, our family. This is personal."

Mario said, "What do you want me to do, Godfather?"

"Nothing visible. Don't brutalize him. His wife will want an open casket. Act nice, bring him candy." He handed Mario a fancy box of chocolates. "...And tie him up, humiliate him, threaten his precious cat. Do whatever you want, but no visible violence."

The next day, when the sign on the front window of the tailor shop said, "Back at 2 PM," Mario, the surgeon, picked the back door's lock.

He was early, and he was starved. Finding a plate of meatballs in Nick's refrigerator, he put them in a small pan and warmed them on the gas stove. Caruso, Nick's long-haired meowing cat, suddenly appeared and rubbed itself against his legs. Mario was agitated. He was violently allergic to cats, and could already see blonde cat hair on his slacks.

He was suddenly itchy, his eyes watered, and hives formed as he brushed cat hair off his pants. Caruso vaulted to the counter near the stove, and in a sudden whoosh, his long hair was aflame. The screeching was unbearable.

Mario suffered a full-blown allergic response. Rubbing his eyes to clear his vision, he threw a dish towel over Caruso, and stabbed the cat repeatedly with the closest thing at hand—Nick's long scissors.

The back room of the tailor shop was a mess. Mario cleaned himself up and took the cover off the pan of meatballs. At least something was perfect. He had no sooner sat down to enjoy his delayed lunch, when he heard Nick unlocking the front door.

"Lock that door behind you, please. I have some candy for you," Mario spoke from the back.

"Wh-wh-what hap-hap-hap-pened in here?" Nick stuttered, as he entered the back room. Then he screamed, "Where is Caruso?"

Mario removed the towel that covered Caruso, so that Nick could see his cat, all the while he was mumbling, "I cooked your meatballs."

All Nick heard was, "I cooked your cat's balls." And he lost his mind. When he saw what was left of Caruso, he had a seizure that tipped over a chair and left him motionless on the floor.

Mario sat down to think... and finish eating.

He was supposed to get the negatives... but now everything was screwed up... how to explain?

He called the Don, and declared, "It's too late for surgery."

"Is he dead?" the Don asked.

"Caca pantaloons... and the cat too."

"Are you wearing gloves?"

"No, but I've wiped everything."

"Get out of there and bring the pictures with you.

A few days later, Marie came home from work and greeted Colleen, who was coloring instead of doing her homework. Marie changed the radio station from rock and roll music to the news, just as their local announcer began.

"Captain DiVito of the Newport Police Department announced the results of the investigation into the death of Nicolas Pastafasio today. The popular tailor died in the back room of his shop on Thames Street, after a struggle with his beloved cat, Caruso, over a pan of meatballs. In the course of the altercation the cat fell into the flames on the stove, and was stabbed nineteen times; the tailor was uninjured. There was no forced entry, and nothing was missing. Mr. Pastafasio's demise was ruled a natural death, caused by a massive heart attack."

Marie called Janet immediately. By coincidence, Veronica and Ana were at the beauty shop. They were elated to hear that Nick was dead. They had both complained about his abuse when they were young. Right then, they decided to celebrate by wearing red to his funeral. It would be their statement.

Janet spread the word to all the ladies who came to the shop, and Nicolas Pastafasio's wake broke all attendance records at the Pagano funeral home. Marie, Colleen, Veronica, Lucia, and Anna went together. Colleen scrutinized Nick in his coffin for any sign of violence, but he looked at peace. She hoped dying hadn't been hard for him. Besides, as her mother reminded her, he was old and would have died soon anyway.

Carmela, who stood beside Nick's wife and daughter to greet the women in red at the church, explained, "My mother is too old to understand, but she is supporting me and every one of you."

They sat on the aisle in the last seat of the last pew of St. Philomena's. When the pallbearers brought Nick's casket up the narrow side steps, Marie could see that they were straining. Tony Balderino definitely looked under the weather. While carrying the coffin down the aisle, without a grunt of warning, he stumbled forward, knocking down old man Cicero who was holding the middle handle.

They both lurched into Mr. Giovanni at the far end. It was a scene from *The Three Stooges at the Crypt.* Suddenly, the pallbearers on the left side were on the floor. The casket landed with a loud crack, the lid popped open, and there was "Uncle Nick" strapped in place, wearing nothing but a diaper like a baby.

The three pallbearers on the right side jumped back and struggled to release their hands to avoid falling into the box. Marie held Colleen tight to block her view. Mrs. Pastafasio's mouth was a shocked circle of lips and teeth. Mourners screamed, and in that moment, almost everyone in the church made the sign of the cross, as though the unholy scene was part of the liturgy. Later, Baldarino said he had taken his medication on an empty stomach. The smell of gin was overpowering in his vicinity.

Once order was restored, the service went like lightning. At the reception, even teetotalers had a drink. It was then that speculation began that Nick's best imported, handmade, Italian suit, the one he wore during the wake, had been stolen. Some said it was divine retribution for the dapper pervert to blast off to eternity wearing nothing but a poop rag. Almost everyone in town ended that day at the Venetian Lounge.

Mrs. Dagostino, the piano teacher, sang traditional Italian songs, the jukebox played Sinatra, and the ladies in red danced until midnight. Under the influence of multiple cocktails, on that strange day, Cousin Anna spoke to Marie about their Uncle Nick.

She said that when she was a child and spoke up about his behavior, she was ridiculed for having an overactive imagination, and when she wouldn't recant, she was punished. She felt guilty for not being more persistent over the years. Marie reminded her that it isn't easy for a child to stand up to adults. "Change happens slow," she said.

Meanwhile, Edward moved back with Marie. He wasn't home a day before Colleen noticed that her Sister Yvonne doll was not on her closet shelf, and she was frantic. Last year when her Aunt Charity came to town, she'd brought the doll in a box with a cellophane window on the front. The doll was exquisitely dressed as a Sister of Saint Joseph nun in a black habit with a stiff white wimple. A cross on a chain around her neck appeared just below the starched white bib covering her shoulders and chest, a black rope circled her waist and hung down the front left side of her long full skirt, with black Rosary beads attached. She looked just like the nuns at St. Joseph's, the school Colleen wanted to attend, but couldn't anymore, because it cost money.

"I'm naming her Sister Yvonne," she said to her aunt. "Where did you find her?"

"She fell off a truck," Charity answered.

Colleen was stunned. There was nothing to indicate an accident of any kind, not even a smudge of road dirt. In order to keep Sister Yvonne perfectly clean, Colleen put her on her closet shelf and took her down to talk to her through the cellophane. Sometimes she took her out to play, then carefully laid her back in the box. Although she looked underneath her skirt, she never undressed Sister Yvonne for fear she wouldn't be able to put her back together correctly. Colleen's only other doll was an old Betsy Wetsy in a cigar box full of sweaters and booties knitted by Marie. Betsy was a doll for little kids. But Sister Yvonne was for big eleven-year-old girls who could take care of special toys.

Marie said, "I can't imagine why your father would move your doll, but we will ask him as soon as he gets home."

Colleen didn't know why her father would have touched her doll either. But every time something bad happened, he was involved. If he had anything to do with the disappearance of Sister Yvonne, she promised herself never to forgive him as long as she lived.

Marie tried to calm her by saying, "*Honor thy father and mother* is one of the commandments. You're jumping to conclusions about your father. That's just like bearing false witness, and there's a commandment about that too, young lady. I think you already owe your father an apology."

But when Edward finally came home, he knew all about Sister Yvonne.

"What do you care? You didn't play with it," he said.

"I played with her all the time," Colleen cried.

"It was still in the box!" he insisted.

"So I could keep her nice! She had already fallen off a truck once! I loved her and I took good care of her!"

"Well, it's gone. I can't do anything about it. You're just carrying on because you're selfish."

"I am not! You stole my doll!"

Edward was angry that this was turning into a federal case. He had been at The Lobster Claw drinking when his buddy, Portuguese Pete, complained that there hadn't been any good junk at the dump lately. As a result he had no birthday present for his daughter. It wasn't that people threw away good gifts, although that happened occasionally, of course. But Portuguese Pete stripped the wires from abandoned appliances and melted them for the copper, which he sold for cash. Pickings had been slim recently; hence he had no way to buy a gift for his little girl. Edward was only trying to do something nice for the kid. He knew Portuguese Pete wasn't much of a father.

It was disappointing that even when he had a good and generous idea, like giving a doll Colleen didn't use to a deserving kid, he was misunderstood and criticized by his own family.

5 Padraig

Padraig made guttural sounds and tugged on people's sleeves to communicate. Where his ears should be, he had lumps of thickened skin on the sides of his head that looked like the squeezed together edges of a pie crust. Despite being constantly rebuffed, he was insistent in his efforts to create words. Like a big puppy that licked the hand that hit him, his gratitude for any kind of attention was annoying, and his enthusiastic forgiveness aggravated his tormentors.

He provoked his father to an extreme level of abuse that upset the whole family. Once, when their mother, Julliette, tried to interfere, he accidentally hit her so hard that after a few days, he had to take her to the hospital. James told the boys that the doctor said their bad behavior caused their mother to have a heart attack, and it was their fault that she died. That was the only explanation he ever gave them for her death.

Padraig's handsome smiling face provoked his father, and other people as well. The teacher in his one-room schoolhouse told Julliette that the special help the boy needed for his deafness was available in Boston. She wrote the name of the clinic and a doctor on a piece of paper. Julliette gave James the teacher's note, and he took a match and set fire to it. When it was almost consumed by the flame, he let it go, and as a few ashes fluttered to the ground he said, "Who does she think I am, Rockefeller?"

Any dope could see for himself what was wrong with his boy. James didn't need some fancy doctor full of fairy dust to pretend that Padraig could be normal. Sure, they could spend a lot of money and the doctor could buy a new Studebaker, but their boy would still be deaf and dumb. James tried to protect his family from a disappointment that would break everyone's heart. It was the least he could do. After all, Padraig's defect was hard for all of them.

No matter, Julliette still sent Padraig to the one-room schoolhouse with his brother Edward and the other children. The teacher had no success teaching him. Padraig was big for his age and rambunctious; neither he nor Edward would sit still. They disrupted everyone by shoving each other, and they spent a lot of time in the corner wearing a dunce's hat.

Their mother wanted them in school, but their father insisted on having their help with farm chores. If James had a field to plow, or corn to get to market, or he needed someone to sell tomatoes from the roadside stand, he kept the boys home. Since the farm was a failure, they only had to work on half of their school days. After Julliette died, James decided they had learned enough. The teacher was relieved when they stopped coming, and the boys were delighted.

Although Padraig had learned little more than how to make his X on an application or contract, he knew how to drive a tractor, and he pretended he could drive other vehicles. He never took a test, or actually had a driver's license, but he drove cars and delivery trucks most of his life without incident.

After losing his eyebrows, he stopped checking the fuel-level by lighting a match and peering into the gas tank. He stayed in a predictable orbit close to home after an excursion into unknown territory trapped him in heavy traffic that stopped completely in front of a busy tunnel. Unable to read the signs around him, he got out of the car and spread a map on the hood to make sense of it. Being deaf, he didn't notice how upset people became when their shouts went unheeded. He was lucky to escape after his illegal U-turn on the grass median when traffic began to move. He learned the hard way that strange places like Providence and the highway to New York were dangerous. He had enough trouble in Somerset.

James O'Leary's ramshackle farm grew smaller as years passed, and fields were leased, or sold. Chickens provided eggs, before they became dinner. The roadside stand moved further away from commerce as the best land was sold. But O'Leary Road still ended at the shore of the Taunton River directly across from the textile mills in Fall River, Mass.

Hanging on to his last business opportunity, James held "Clambakes" for the factory workers on "O'Leary's Beach." Running bakes was more lucrative than farming anyway, especially when James added to his coffers by turning part of the barn into a bar and gaming room. He sold "home brew" in canning jars, and beer from a keg.

Card games filled a corner of the barn with loud bets and curses. Men played horseshoes beside the barn, and baseball in the field. Women wandered down to the shore to swim, and sat on blankets with a beer or soda. It was hot as Hades during the summer in the mills, and the annual clambakes, partially funded by mill owners, were a popular outing. The boys ferried the mill-hands, mostly young women, back and forth in a skiff with a small motor.

Their father made Padraig and Edward start the day by clearing a place in front of the barn where large round rocks were covered with wood and set ablaze. The boys went to the beach to gather baskets of seaweed while James, the bake-master, barked orders. Lollygagging resulted in a cuff on the side of the head.

When the red-hot stones were raked clear of wood, the bake-master added a fresh layer of seaweed. Mill workers watched through clouds of steam as wire baskets of onions, potatoes, eggs, corn on the cob, sausage, hotdogs, chorizo, clams, and finally lobsters were placed on top and covered with a tarp. Rocks around the perimeter sealed the steam inside. Picnic tables were covered with butcher paper and cups readied for melted butter and clam broth.

Everyone drank a lot of beer, and before the day was over there was usually a fight. Drunken men in the barn formed a circle surrounding the fighters, who were also tipsy. Men pushed each other around and fell onto the sawdust-covered floor. Spectators wagered money on the winner, if there was time to bet before someone passed out.

Neighbors were not close enough to be disturbed by the shouting, so there was little chance of a complaint. One of James' friends wandered around with a nightstick hanging from a loop on his overalls and a fake "Constable" badge. He worked for beer, all he could drink, and his presence kept things from getting out of hand.

With a quiet confidence that impressed everyone, including his father, Edward ran the boat that ferried the girls back to Fall River. Padraig tended a bonfire on the beach and roasted marshmallows for them while they waited for their ride. He was older than Edward and big for his age. The proximity of young attractive factory workers overwhelmed him.

Padraig had watched the girls earlier in the afternoon when they came out of the water after swimming. As they toweled themselves dry, he observed undulating movements beneath the fabric of their bathing suits, which suggested soft rosy flesh he could only imagine. Now, around the bonfire at dusk, one of the young women, tipsy from beer and emboldened by the crowd of girls around her, flirted with him. It was an innocent game of "Show-Off Teases the Dunce" that everyone enjoyed.

Padraig was tall, well-built, and had a healthy tan from outdoor work. In an attempt to please, he nodded as though he understood, even when he did not. His bright, even smile and dimples were engaging. Dark, thick hair covered his ears most of the time and at first glance, he looked to be a fine physical specimen.

The drunken girl and her friends knew he was deaf and had seen how failure in his efforts to communicate only made him more determined. On many occasions during the long hot day, they had been shocked to see that his father's merciless rebukes had provoked no angry response.

They couldn't believe it. It was as though his appearance, which was the opposite of his abilities, created an additional annoyance of disappointed expectations. Unable to understand why, they wanted to push the envelope and make him lash out. He disturbed them. Unable to understand what he had done to make the girls mad, he was confused.

A brash girl, more drunk than the others, teased him as he stood by the fire in his bathing clothes. She smiled and looked up into his eyes as though they shared a secret; then she looked down at his hand holding a stick with a toasted marshmallow on its tip. Taking a step closer, she placed her hand over his on the stick. Gazing into his eyes again, she used her other hand to steady the end of the stick while bringing her lips down to the marshmallow, slowly licking it before taking it into her mouth.

Padraig, so close he could see the golden hairs in her ears, the hint of sweat on her forehead, and a few shiny grains of sand on her cheek, held his breath for fear his slightest movement would make her go away. She pulled her head back as though the marshmallow was too hot. "Wow, that's good," she said looking at the other girls.

They all laughed as she bent to lick the marshmallow again before putting her mouth over it. This time when she pulled her head back, the marshmallow was gone. Padraig's sharp intake of breath was audible. The girl looked at him and said, "More!"

Overtired, overfed, and full of beer, the other girls laughed as though eating a marshmallow was hilarious. Uncomfortable at the center of their attention, Padraig also laughed and blushed deeply, then bent to put another marshmallow on the stick. When he stood up to put the stick near the fire, the girls' laughter increased. He saw a few of them wiping their eyes and speaking to each other behind hands they held in front of their mouths. He saw her point at his Mr. Johnson.

Instinct told him to run away and hide, but speed was out of the question. Besides, if he left the fire, his father would beat him. The girl stepped closer to him and smiled as she pointed to her open mouth.

"More," she yelled. Padraig knew she was shouting because her mouth was so big.

The shrillness of the girl's tone attracted his father to the bonfire. James saw the situation in an instant. Padraig expected to be knocked senseless. Instead, his father took the stick from his hand and pushed him away.

"Go!" he ordered while turning to offer the toasted marshmallow to the girl. "This one's ready for you, little lady," he said. "I'm taking over here."

James smiled at her and reached into his pocket to retrieve a flask of whiskey, which he held out, and she accepted.

Padraig disappeared into the dusk. He needed to be alone.

The crowd in the barn paid no attention as he climbed the ladder to the loft, seeking the darkest spot he knew. In the shadows of the far corner something moved. Fighting tears, his eyes adjusted and he saw a man almost on top of a girl. The man had his mouth near the girl's ear as though he was whispering to her while he pulled his pants down low on his legs. The girl's skirt was being pushed up and her blouse was mostly off.

He knew he'd be in a lot of trouble if he didn't get out of there before he was noticed. But he would need to take his eyes off the skirt and the legs in order to relocate the ladder. Unable to look away, and afraid that a move would make noise, Padraig stood still as a statue.

Although the man and girl were busy, something made the man look over his shoulder. With a mad face he said, "Get out of here!"

Padraig didn't hear the words, but he stumbled back and flung himself down the ladder.

Upon seeing him in a blur, the bartender waved to catch his attention and held up a bottle of beer. "Padraig, come on over here and wet your whistle. You look like you need a drink."

He definitely needed a drink. He drained it and was just starting his second when the man who had been in the loft appeared at his elbow. Padraig recognized Frisco, who ran a jazz club in the city, and had a reputation as a lady's man.

Frisco immediately took two beers and pulled Padraig outside to an empty table. The boy bowed his head and covered his face with shaking hands. Frisco's anger evaporated upon observing the cowering rube. "Don't cry," he said, as he placed a bottle of beer in front of Padraig.

"Poor dumb Mick," he muttered. "His whole life is going to be nothing but hard work and disappointment. People will always make fun of him, and take advantage of him. There's no way he'll ever get a woman to give him anything but a slap in the face and a cold shoulder. He deserves something."

Before they finished their next beers, Frisco said, "I'm going to give you a secret weapon that will change your life. It is my best line, words I have never told anyone else. These five words should be whispered close to a woman's ear. They should be said soft. You can say 'Please,' first or last, but you must always say please. These words are the secret of my success with women, which I am sure even a dope like you has heard about. Since you will never be able to say them, I'm writing them down for you. Just give this piece of paper to a girl, and wait for the magic."

Padraig understood little of what Frisco said, but he nodded with pleasure as he held the paper. They both had another beer, and Frisco slapped Padraig on the back and went to play poker.

Holding the paper, Padraig ventured down the lane to the beach. It had been a very emotional day and he had consumed more beer than he'd ever had in his life. He was suddenly exhausted. The bonfire on the beach was low, and only a few people waited to be ferried back to Fall River. When he saw an abandoned blanket in the sand, he sat down and pulled it up around his shoulders.

A girl hurrying down the beach toward the boat landing didn't see him, and tripped over his feet. Grabbing his outstretched hand, she steadied herself before taking a closer look. It was the girl who had been with Frisco in the loft.

"You!" She gasped, and raised her hand to slap him.

Padraig couldn't control his emotions any longer. He started to cry because the girl who wanted more marshmallows had mocked him. And his despair gathered momentum as he remembered how the whole crowd of girls made fun of him. Now he was dizzy from all the beer, and the girl from the loft wanted to hit him! Worst of all, he would never be able to read the special paper from Frisco.

Stunned, the girl didn't strike him. She knelt on the blanket and began to cry with him. She cried because her clothes had been half off while this deaf boy watched Frisco touching her, and because this kid and Frisco had been laughing about her, and because her head ached, and she hated her job in the mill, and she was homesick for the farm, and she detested the city, and she had nowhere else to go.

Finally, she cried because she'd never been able to see someone else cry without crying too. Even as a child, she had shed more tears for others than on her own account. They sat together on the blanket and wept until they stopped. Then she took a handkerchief from her pocket and wiped her nose. "Let me see that paper he gave you," she said as she reached over and took the note away from him.

Bending toward the dying fire she read, "Please put me inside you."

"That *creep!*" she said, remembering how Frisco murmured those words against her neck just before the kid showed up. When Padraig saw her angry eyes full of tears, he lowered his head to his hands and began to cry again.

"You poor slob," she said as she put her arms around him and smoothed his hair. She petted him, and calmed him, and hugged him. She scrunched down so they could both stretch out to be more comfortable. While they held each other, she pulled the blanket up around them and stroked him as though he were a brokenhearted child. His sniffling persisted.

Encouraged by her continued efforts to comfort him, he touched her hair and neck and kissed her ear, loving her tentatively, going where instinct led. She synchronized herself to the rhythm around her, until suddenly Padraig was in a little home where he had never

56

been so warm. His body shook as his heart beat through his body like sound vibrating through a crowd. He was sweating and hot; hot everywhere. Then something happened and finally he could catch his breath.

Resting in her arms he wondered what her name was. He wanted to know the name of the girl he loved with his whole heart. He tried to ask her, but she wasn't used to the way he spoke, and shushed him by placing her finger on his lips. She didn't seem too tired to hug him some more, and he was glad. When they were quiet, he wondered which one of them had the note; he didn't want to lose it. He wanted to give it to this girl every day for the rest of his life. Then he fell into a deep sleep.

Still a little tipsy, she muttered, "Crap, I can never go to another clambake," and caught the last boat to Fall River.

6 ADELINE

Until now, Adeline's worst transgression had been skipping mass, but the previous night something bad had happened. Although her mother thought she was still a good girl, Adeline had wantonly done the sex act, without the sanctity of marriage. Geographical distance protected her for the moment, but when her mother saw her face, she would immediately know she was a hussy who had fallen from grace.

She couldn't lie to her mother in her Sunday letter, but she couldn't tell the truth either. She had not actually said she was going to church every Sunday, but she didn't reveal that she wasn't. By the time she selected words to create the correct misunderstanding—which is to say the precise words to ease her mother's mind by omitting the truth—her head ached from the duplicity, in addition to her hangover.

Due to the anonymity of the big city, she barely knew a soul at the mill in Fall River. Only Frisco and the earless boy were aware of her moral failure. Her head throbbed with images that made her groan aloud. As the hours passed, her misery and torment increased. Remembering details of the previous night, she became morose. The dishonesty of her upstanding appearance rebuked her when she looked in the mirror. If only it were a bad dream and nothing had really happened.

However, after years of avoiding occasions of sin with boys whose hands tried to wander, she had done the inconceivable, the worst thing possible. When her mind revisited the clambake, recalling events in the hayloft, and in the blanket on the beach, her head dropped in disgrace. It was hard to believe, but she might have done the sex act twice.

Last night she had been different from her normal self. Feeling no shame, she had lost her moral compass and gone astray. Now she would never meet a nice boy and get married in white. After all, who would marry a girl who possibly had sex, not twice with one man, but *once* with *two* men... at the same clambake?

Adeline was a loose woman. Her future was uncertain, and she was terrified. What rules controlled the newly depraved? Losing her virginity was confusing. She didn't know if she had really done it with Frisco. It was definitely possible, but she wasn't sure because it was her first time, and she hadn't known what to expect. There seemed to be some difficulty, and there was the interruption in the hayloft, but it might have happened a little bit. It was a technical issue.

But she had definitely, oh yes, she definitely had sex with the earless one. Needless to say, she would never allow herself to see him again. And it was a sort of a mercy-sex, like something a nun would do as her final good deed, for a special dispensation, if the world were coming to an end. She needed to go to confession right away, and she needed to get a new scapular, and wear it until she died a miserable old maid. She prayed about her weekend of debauchery, and she prayed to find a new job. Her life was ruined.

Drinking beer was at the heart of her fall; it put her in a mental fog, and led her to trust Frisco. What a disastrous mistake. Frisco delivered hot meals to the lunchroom at the mill, and always chatted up the floor manager, her boss. Adeline had heard Frisco was a "ladies man" and had refused his invitations. But one day her boss called to her while Frisco was standing right beside him. He reminded her that each of the mill workers could bring a guest to the clambake, and suggested that since Frisco wanted to go, it would be nice if she asked him. Embarrassed and put on the spot, she said, "Okay."

Frisco said, "Great!"

It happened so fast she didn't know how to stop it. She was trapped.

The long, hot day of games, swimming, and heavy food enhanced the refreshing qualities of cold beer. Unaccustomed to drinking alcohol, Adeline overdid it and became intoxicated. Homesick and lonely, she turned into a drunken hussy. Now she didn't know what she would do when she saw Frisco, except possibly die. And how could she ever face her boss or the other girls again? Dropping to her knees, she prayed that she, and those she had been with, would lose all memory of the clambake, forever and ever, Amen.

Two months later she was sick with a persistent stomach flu. One of the girls at rooming house said, "You're not pregnant, are you?"

At first, she was insulted, but when she thought back to the clambake, she knew it was possible. A few weeks later, her suspicions were confirmed, and she cried nonstop. Tearfully, she told her boss that her mother was seriously ill, and she must return home before it was too late. After packing her suitcase with everything she had brought to the city, she took a bus to Attleboro.

Her mother and father, who thought she had a few days off, met her at the station. On the ride home while they filled her in on the latest farm news, Adeline was quiet, and preoccupied. Once inside her own warm kitchen she reached into the cupboard for her favorite mug. Making a cup of tea filled her with emotions fueled by hormones. Because her anxiety was at the tipping point, she began to weep, which led to sobs, and then hiccoughs. In between onslaughts, she told her parents the truth, or her version.

She spoke of the hot day and the many beers consumed. She explained that she had been vulnerable and lonely and drunk, and now she didn't know what to do. Her parents were inconsolable; they paced, cried, and asked if she was sure, again and again. Her mother said she'd never be able to face the neighbors, and her father said she didn't have the sense of a turnip.

Adeline hadn't mentioned the earless dunce when she threw herself at her parents' feet and begged for their help. When her father wanted to make Frisco marry her, she insisted that she wouldn't marry him; he hadn't even come to Mrs. Joubert's rooming house to say hello after the clambake. They put on their coats and took a walk to clear their heads while they tried to think.

Adeline's mother, Dottie, thought of her sister Janet whose husband died in his sleep when their son Wayne was only two years old. Janet had opened a small beauty shop in the basement of her home in Swansea and seemed to be making ends meet. Dottie decided to ask for her help. During a lengthy phone call, the sisters formulated a plan. Adeline would live with Janet, help to care for Wayne, and apprentice in the shop.

Janet agreed to explain Adeline's situation in advance of her arrival by saying that her niece's brand-new husband died in a tractor accident while helping his brother on the family farm during harvest. Shortly after the funeral, Adeline became too sick to go to work, and discovered she was pregnant. Unable to afford the rent for their city apartment on her own, she quit her job in Fall River and moved home.

Embellishing further, Janet would say that when she heard that her favorite niece was a young widow with a baby on the way, she was sympathetic. She knew firsthand the difficult road ahead, and she was pleased when her sister Dottie Frazier asked her to teach Adeline to be a beautician. Her sister and brother-in-law had been good to her when her husband died, and she wanted to return the favor. Besides, she could use a few extra hands. She welcomed Adeline's energy and good humor. Wayne loved to play with her because she was like a kid herself.

The story sounded plausible, and they all agreed to keep it simple, avoiding details. Janet had been lonely since her husband's death. Being busy with a toddler, and working in her own home, had kept her virtually house bound. She only had two types of customers and both drove her nuts. The first was boring and old, and the second was old and dead. The local funeral home called her regularly. Her niece's company promised to bring a ray of sunshine.

Adeline soon learned a new way to comb hair. "All forward from the rear." Dead or alive, old women seemed to have scraggly hair that needed to be forced to the front and fluffed up around the face. Her customers didn't turn to see the back of their heads and Janet didn't encourage that foolishness by holding up a mirror.

The live ones were pleased with the full soft look that Adeline created. As for the dead, she was careful to keep their bodies flat after a bad experience when she turned a woman's head too far while adjusting her side curls. The woman rolled completely off the gurney, and although Adeline tried desperately to roll her back, it was hopeless.

She had to make an emergency call to her Aunt Janet, who rushed to the funeral home with a bathing board. It took all of their combined strength to leverage the woman onto the gurney again. They were both sweaty and done-in by the time the corpse was back in place with her hair fixed and make-up applied.

Aunt Janet had a theatrical flair that made everything seem special. She taught Adeline to give long, gentle shampoos, finished with a soothing head massage. While a towel soaked in hot water, Janet prepared her individual revitalizing, moisturizing treatment. Unscented conditioner bought in bulk awaited her magic in a large crock. She consulted the formula on a recipe card before ladling a small amount into a measuring cup. Then, as careful as a pharmacist, she added a little aloe from an eye dropper, and a spoonful of eucalyptus oil. After rubbing the fragrant concoction onto a woman's wet scalp, she wound a hot towel tightly around her head.

Janet lowered the back of her customer's chair to a reclining position and said, "Breathe deeply and close your eyes." Sounds of contentment filled the tiny shop. When the egg timer rang, the towel was unwrapped, and the hair was washed and rinsed again. Janet's "Hot Oil Rescue" and other treatments were quite popular. She encouraged Adeline to sell them, and paid her a bonus when she did.

After years of conversation with women who were sitting under a hair dryer louder than an industrial vacuum, Janet's voice was shrill. When she laughed, its volume increased until her cackle could drown out the siren on a fire engine. Regardless of how it suited her, she always wore her hair in the latest style.

When Mia Farrow cut her hair into a pixie, Janet immediately cut hers and Adeline's to match. A self-proclaimed expert on the pixie, she slicked down her platinum locks and carefully positioned them around her forehead like Julius Caesar's on an old Roman coin.

Janet told her customers that they would not only look more youthful in a pixie, they would find it simple to manage. She boasted that it had been "Voted the most flattering hairdo in a decade by the Hairdressers' Association," and promised that it didn't flatten, even after romance. Winking and hooting before making that last statement, she added, "I think that's why Mia got it."

She often suggested, "Take off those heavy boots so that I can wrap your feet in a towel and rest them on this hot water bottle. It will make you feel better." Janet was hard to resist, and she was always selling. Straightforward, sideways, or around the back door, she was always seeking to close the sale. Once her prey was disarmed by the hot water bottle, or special herb tea, she was back in business.

"How about a pixie, Josephine? Are you ready for adventure?"

Janet purchased several large tubes of Brylcream at the pharmacy and squeezed it into tiny glass jars labeled "Pixie Magic." When the old ladies saw Adeline with her new pixie haircut, carrying a basket of pixie cream, she looked as fresh as a fairy princess ready to be ravished by a charming prince. Everyone raved.

"A jar of pixie-magic is our free gift to everyone who gets this haircut," Janet said. Josephine, Bertha, Frances, and Edwina had a pixie cut before the week was over. When Janet told them they hadn't looked this good in years, she was convincing. Later when they were unsure, they remembered her next statement.

"When you get up in the morning and see yourself in the mirror, you'll think you made a mistake. People always feel that way when they've made a change, even a change for the better. Just notice how many people mention your new haircut. That will show you the truth."

She twirled around with her back arched so that she could keep sight of herself in the mirror. At the end of her spin, she re-adjusted her bangs. Janet was thirty-nine years old and lean, with large features, heavy eyebrows, a prominent nose, and a wide smile of big teeth. Her hair was unusually thick; it embraced her head like a shiny pelt to be ruffled and smoothed. Like a grape, Janet's skin was taut with juice... she was the physical opposite of her customers. They were raisins, with pixie hair rested atop their spotted skulls, like spikes of dried grass on bumpy new graves. Unfortunately, they looked older with the pixie-cut, and balder. But before they realized that, Janet had convinced them to grow their hair back.

Meticulously becoming the master of every craft that came along, Janet crocheted plant hangers, slippers with fancy tassels, and monogrammed placemats. She created stunning "Cape Cod" purses with imitation scrimshaw embellishments, and much more. The shop was the perfect place to sell handmade gifts. Adeline and Janet were a good team, and business prospered. Women sympathetic to Adeline's predicament followed Janet's advice to keep her cheerful by being cheerful themselves. They avoided mention of Adeline's late husband, and Janet's too, for that matter.

Several months after she had moved to Swansea, Adeline was shocked when she answered the front door to find Frisco standing on the stoop. He had spoken to her boss and when he found that she had left abruptly to take care of her sick mother, and he had visited her rooming house. There he convinced Mrs. Joubert to give him her parents' address. He had immediately driven to the farm and met her mother and father. Glad to find her mother recovered, he begged her parents for Adeline's address. When they relented, he drove right over.

He said he was sorry that he had not been in touch with her after the clambake. His father died in New York that night and he left to be with his mother as soon as he found out. He had been helping her since then. She was resettled now, and he was ready to get back to his own life. His father's death had wakened him to the passage of time and importance of settling down and starting his own family.

Noticing her expanding waistline, he asked if she was pregnant. She nodded yes. He asked if the loft was her first sexual experience. Again, she nodded yes. He said he thought so, and he wanted to have a chance to be a father to their baby. He was tired of avoiding responsibility, and sick of running around. He wanted to marry her and take care of his family; he was ready.

Adeline was stunned. His sincerity impressed her. Getting married would be the right thing in her condition. It was certainly the best thing for the baby. Frisco wanted her to leave with him, but something held her back. She said she needed time to think.

When her parents and Aunt Janet heard that Frisco wanted to marry her, they were ecstatic; and when Adeline told them that she had turned him down, they were furious. But she was steadfast in her response that she wasn't in love with him, and wouldn't marry someone she didn't love.

They began to see each other. When the old ladies at the beauty shop wanted details, she explained that Frisco was a close friend of her dead husband, who felt sorry for her. He visited her every Sunday, a time they both anticipated and enjoyed. They became good friends, and before he left, he often whispered in her ear, "Come with me right now. Let's elope."

She always laughed and said, "Maybe next week."

If the day ended and he hadn't asked her to leave with him, she thought, "I would have gone if he asked me today." But they were never of the same mind at the same time. She called him when she went into labor. Her parents had already spent a few anxious hours in the waiting room by the time Frisco arrived. They gave him a hug and said Adeline was already under anesthesia.

When the baby was born, she was very small and slow to cry. The doctor turned to the nurse and said, "Bilateral microtia," before heading to the waiting room to talk to her parents.

Adeline was still groggy when the doctor led her parents and Frisco to the nursery, where they watched through the window as the baby turned her head. They saw the tiny flaps of crinkled skin where her ears should be. In every other way, the tiny girl was beautiful.

The doctor said, "Your baby was born without ears."

He asked Dot and Frank if a family member had a similar deformity. Then he turned to Frisco and asked if he had any relatives without ears. Pale and shaken, he replied, "I'm not the baby's father."

Adeline's mother quickly jumped in. "Our daughter is a widow, doctor."

"I'm sorry," the doctor said. "My mistake, I'm really sorry."

He turned to Frisco. "I'll have to ask you to excuse us, while I discuss the baby with her family."

Frisco didn't utter a word, but when he looked at the Fraziers, his eyes were swimming. He ran out of the hospital just as Adeline woke up. Her parents were solemn when the doctor asked Adeline if anyone in her husband's family had been born without ears.

She blanched, and there was a slight tremor of her hand as she pulled the coverlet up.

"No," she said. "I know of no one."

Convinced that her innocent baby was being punished for her sins, Adeline was devastated. When the doctor explained Amberjean's birth defect, Adeline's parents struggled to understand the problems that lie ahead. And although Adeline regretted her past mistakes, she was glad she had refused to marry Frisco.

Examining the baby as he spoke, the doctor said something had gone wrong in her development. He began, "At this point it is impossible to know if the interior ear canals are intact. Your baby will need surgery eventually, but nothing can be done until her bones are more developed."

The doctor said, "Ninety percent of children with microtia have one working ear. Having both ears affected makes things more difficult. But if the ear canal and the small bones are in place, there is a good chance that someday she will have nearly perfect hearing. The most difficult time will be when she is a small child, unable to hear, and unable to communicate.

"Corrective surgeries can begin when she is six or seven and her bones have grown enough to be used to create ears by carving them from her rib cartilage. Using her own tissue eliminates the problem of rejection. The ears will be placed under her skin on the sides of her face. Later surgery will lift the bones up, and project them from the side of the head."

The doctor pointed out that girls were lucky to be able to hide their ears with long hair. The problem was worse for boys because their deformity was visible, and it made them victims of teasing.

Reconstruction was going to take a minimum of four operations, and the new ear wouldn't grow like the rest of the child; it would appear too large... until she grew into it. By the time microtia had been surgically corrected and hearing established, the damage of teasing was usually significant.

The information was too much for Adeline to absorb. She could not bear the thought of a surgeon cutting her child's flesh and poking around inside her skull to look for an ear canal. The doctor had not mentioned the cost of all this, and Adeline couldn't ask. It was too much to know.

Aunt Janet said, "Concentrate on the present and let the future take care of itself. You have your hands full right now. Worry about all of that later." That was the best advice she received, and Adeline followed it.

Amberjean was a happy baby, a precious gift to her mother, and a blessing to the old women who frequented the shop as well as her Aunt Janet, and her cousin Wayne. She was two years old before things changed. Janet fell in love with a widower, and agreed to marry him and raise his three children. Their marriage would mean that Janet would no longer have room for Adeline and Amberjean in her home. She would close the shop to the general public and limit her skill to members of her own family.

Adeline would have to go to beauty school if she intended to continue as a beautician, but she really was not interested. She was tired of finger waves and pin-curls. An article about Cardinal Spellman's New York Foundling Hospital's one-year program to train infant and childcare technicians captured her attention.

For a small tuition fee, the hospital provided board and instruction five days a week. Graduates were certified to work as delivery room nurses who care for babies right after birth, a job that would allow Adeline to support Amberjean. She applied immediately and was accepted. Her parents agreed to take care of their granddaughter during Adeline's year of nurse's training. Although it would break her heart to leave Amberjean temporarily, the promise of future independence made the sacrifice acceptable.

On the appointed day, Adeline kissed Amberjean goodbye and boarded a bus to New York. Before the sun had set, she had been welcomed by her roommate, Regina Feldson, who helped her move into their small room at the hospital.

Adeline loved the blue uniforms with stiffly starched white collars and cuffs that were delivered to her closet once a week. With barely a moment to herself, she worked, studied, and wrote a few lines or drew a picture for Amberjean every night. At the end of each week, she sent an envelope home.

A ten o'clock curfew was strictly enforced, and her two days off were rarely together, or on a weekend. Organized, productive and challenged, there were no extra moments; except for missing Amberjean, she had never been happier.

Arriving home for Easter, Adeline was stunned by how much her daughter had changed. Amberjean had been a silent child who babbled infrequently and unintelligibly. But now, she turned the pages of her book, and made noises like she understood every word she was reading to the dolls lined up on her bed.

When someone called, "Come see what we have for Amberjean," they all trouped out the back door. Dottie had a large basket with a pink bow on the handle, and when she bent down to show Amberjean a puppy, the child clapped her hands and jumped up and down with excitement,

Clear as a bell she said, "Ammadaa, Ammadaa."

Suddenly Adeline understood. Amberjean was calling her grandmother "Mama Dot," just like everyone else did.

When she held up her arms to ask her grandfather to pick her up, she said, "PaMa, PaMa."

After that, Adeline began to observe her daughter more carefully. She could see that Amberjean became impatient and frustrated when her efforts were ignored or misunderstood. Adeline vowed to learn as much as she could to help her daughter communicate. When Amberjean kissed her and said, "Amma," Adeline thought "momma" had never sounded sweeter. She knew that helping her child to speak was the most important thing she would ever do.

On their day off they sometimes took the subway to Sunnyside to be with her roommate Regina's family. Having a serious boyfriend kept Regina in the dorm with her books. Like Adeline, Regina rarely went out with the rest of the girls to movies, parties, and clubs. They weren't much younger than Adeline, but they were more carefree.

That's why it came as a surprise to everyone when Regina agreed to go to Cape Cod with them for Fourth of July. She even persuaded Adeline to come along. They planned to leave after their last shift on Tuesday night, and didn't have to be back until Friday at ten p.m.

When her boyfriend called at the last minute to say he was coming home, Regina canceled. The other girls persuaded Adeline to go anyway. They sang and told stories all night while they drove. Arriving in Hyannis exhausted, they checked into a motel and went to bed. It was early afternoon when they woke up and went out for breakfast, before going to the beach. Stretching out on towels in the sand, most of them fell asleep again. Everyone was sunburned.

That night, with faces hot and red, they went to a small low-ceilinged bar in Osterville. They drank beer and danced together around the jukebox. Soon, a large group of boys from St. John's in the city joined them, and everyone danced in a circle.

When Adeline finally sat down, a boy nearby asked her if she wanted to go to a party. She said, "Yes," and asked him if he went to St. John's too. "Yes," was his reply. She told her friends she would be back in a little while, and went with the boy to his car. They hadn't driven a block when another boy sat up in the back seat. The driver was not surprised. He did not introduce, or speak to the one in the back.

Interrupting the silence of the thundercloud in the car, Adeline said, "I have to go back. It's too late for me to go anywhere now, and my friends will want to leave soon."

No response.

They drove for what seemed like a long time. The air in the car was too heavy to breathe. There were no streetlights, no shops, no gas stations, no people. No place to jump out. No place to run, if she did jump. No person to run to. No cars behind them, or in front. Nothing.

She begged first one, and then the other to take her back, but her pleading made no difference. They ignored it, the way they ignored her. Neither spoke at all. It was as if she was invisible. The road was pitch black; the only light outside was from the headlights on the pavement directly in front of them. Inside, the driver's profile was lit by a greenish glow from the dashboard. When he glanced sideways, empty black holes, where his eyes should have been, looked in her direction but did not see her.

Adeline heard her voice become frantic, but it did not penetrate the air or reach them. They remained unresponsive to her, and didn't speak to each other. Finally, they turned off the paved road onto a dirt one, and stopped in front of a beach shack. The driver opened the door with a key. Adeline thought briefly of refusing to move, but abandoned the idea.

She was afraid that if she didn't move, they would reach in to pull her out, and once they started there would be no stopping it... no stopping them. When they went inside, she followed.

The one from the back seat took something from a refrigerator and heated it on the stove. He stood with a spoon and ate out of the pan. The other made two drinks. He brought one to where she stood and put it down on a table beside her. He returned to the counter with his. Adeline didn't touch the drink, but when she looked around and thought, *Where is the party?* one of them said, "Soon. The party will start soon," as if he had heard her.

I will die here, she thought as she went to the screen door and looked out at nothing but the black, impenetrable, hopeless night.

She seemed to be detached from her body, in the air near the ceiling, looking down at the back of her head and over her shoulder into the empty void beyond the door. Then she heard a sound she didn't recognize at first. It was her own voice, different than it had ever sounded before, whimpering, and babbling prayers out loud, calling to Jesus for help.

A small red light appeared at the edge of her peripheral vision, and moved. Adeline bolted through the screen door screaming "Help! Help!" again and again.

She must have jumped over a hedge because she was suddenly running toward the red light on the roof of a police car. The car stopped and she jumped in. The policeman asked, "What happened?"

Adeline was cold with fear, shivering.

"What happened?" the policeman said again. "Did anybody touch you?"

She saw she was only wearing one shoe, and she had no idea when the other fell off. "No," she answered, no one had touched her.

The policeman told her he was driving around because there were rumors of girls being raped in a beach shack. "...Right here in Truro."

He said he had to stay in his area, and he took her back to the border of Osterville, and pointed out her motel, just across the street. He watched while she walked across and entered the room where the girls waited.

They told her they had gone back to the motel when the bar closed. They were very worried about her. The boy she had left with wasn't known by any of the boys from St. John's. The bartender thought he might have seen him before, and he might be a volunteer fireman, but he wasn't sure.

Morning was just a few hours away. The girls had another night at the Cape ahead of them, they looked forward to more beer, more dancing, more fun. Adeline told them she would get the first bus in the morning. They could not talk her into staying. They were still asleep when she left a note and walked to the bus station with her suitcase.

After buying a ticket to Providence with a transfer to Attleboro, she relaxed a little. She wanted to be home more than anything. She didn't want to be a nurse, or take care of anyone else's baby; she wanted to be with her own baby, and never leave home again. For the rest of her life, Adeline checked the back seat every time she entered a car. Her basic belief in the fundamental decency of fellow human beings was shattered.

Surprised and happy when Adeline called to say she was coming home, her mother and father picked her up at the bus station. An ecstatic Amberjean sat in her lap on the way to the farm. Adeline told her parents that she had gone to the Cape with the girls at the end of their shift on Tuesday, and had been there for a whole day and overnight. Her classmates were still there, she said, but she was too lonely to remain.

She didn't mention the cottage, or the boys who took her there, or the policeman who had probably saved her life. She said she had been thinking of Amberjean and the farm for some time. Too miserable to continue in school, she said she no longer wanted to be a childcare technician. Firm in her resolve, she vowed she would find another way to support herself.

"Is the school work too hard?" her father wanted to know.

"No, I can do it," she said.

"Are they mean to you?" her mother wondered.

"No."

"Adeline, we don't understand."

"You should trust me to do what is best for Amberjean," she insisted. Adeline could not understand why strangers like the boys at the cottage had wanted to hurt her. She didn't feel competent to protect herself and Amberjean from danger. If her parents took care of them, and sheltered them, they might be safe for a while on the farm. She never told them about that night.

Her parents were stunned by this unexpected turn of events. But Adeline was serious. "I need to go back to the residence to get my things. Will you take me?" she asked.

"We promised your Aunt Janet we would help her move today. Wayne is looking forward to playing with Amberjean. You stay home and think about what you're doing. We'll take Amberjean with us because they will be disappointed if we don't. We'll talk to you when we get back." Her parents were quiet in their disappointment. The subject was closed. They left her alone and continued on with their granddaughter as planned.

After unpacking, Adeline wrote a letter of resignation to the Director of the school and put it in her empty suitcase. She didn't expect her parents to drive her back to New York to get her things. They only helped her when she did what they wanted. On her own now, she made a cup of tea and left them a note. Then she started the long walk to the bus stop. At least the empty suitcase was light.

She rode the bus to New York as she had on the day that she moved into the hospital residency, only this time she wasn't excited; she was scared. Her classmates weren't due back until the following night. With any luck, the dorm would be empty.

Slipping the letter under the door of the Administrative Office, she hurried to her room to pack. Thank God, Regina wasn't there. Adeline did not want to see anyone, and certainly not someone who would object to her moving out, and ask her to explain the unexplainable. It was better that her parents weren't with her. Their presence would have attracted attention.

As she struggled to close her suitcase, a nurse knocked on the door to say that the Director, Miss Sutherlin, expected Adeline in her office immediately.

"Come in and sit down, Adeline." Miss Sutherlin's smile had no round edges. She was as stiff as her uniform. "What's wrong? And don't lie to me."

Adeline started to cry.

"Anyone who makes up a husband, has a baby with a deformity, and keeps it all a secret, shouldn't cry when asked a simple question."

Adeline looked up. "How?"

"Sometimes information comes to me indirectly. Bilateral microtia is an unusual condition. A doctor from Swansea might contact an old friend from medical school whose specialty is pediatric corrective surgery. He might ask his friend about new developments in treatment and reconstruction. That friend might be a surgeon new to our staff, who might chat with me about a child whose mother is at the Foundling Hospital Nursing School in New York. It's just a thought."

Adeline was speechless.

"Here's another thought. How much do you think your schooling has cost? Do you really think it is free? It's not. It's subsidized. Did you realize that you might have to pay it back if you quit? Do you know you could be required to work here without salary until your debt is satisfied?"

She felt her face flush. "What about Julie Coskie? She was allowed to quit."

Miss Sutherlin smacked her lips. "She flunked out. That's different."

There was a long silence, and Miss Sutherlin waited for Adeline to absorb it.

"How much?" Adeline asked.

"A lot, several thousand!"

Adeline looked stricken.

"You are four months from graduation and you are ranked third in your class. This is an opportunity that you can't repeat. Your future and that of your child will be vastly different without this education."

"What can I do?"

"You can take your suitcase back to your room and unpack. You can help in delivery tonight. We are shorthanded. Then you can report to work tomorrow at eleven p.m. as scheduled, with the rest of your class. You are twenty-one, Adeline, an adult who is legally responsible for her debts. A helpless child depends on you. It's a good thing I didn't see this letter. Take it back.

"I've been doing this long enough to be sure of my ability to pick students. You are where you are meant to be, and you are doing what you are supposed to be doing. I know it. We will not mention this again. You can come to talk to me anytime, but not about quitting. Do you understand?"

Miss Sutherlin squeezed her narrow lips as she handed the letter back to Adeline and stood up to leave.

Adeline stood also. When she and the valise were back in her room, she sat on the bed and looked at it. She was exhausted. Stretching out for a moment to collect her thoughts, she fell into a deep sleep and that's where she was when Regina came in a few hours later.

7 CHARITY

Edward had been in the doghouse since he gave Colleen's Sister-Yvonne doll away. He called his half-sister Charity in New York, collect, and when he told her everyone was on his case, his voice cracked.

"Edward, do you want me to come and see you?" she asked.

"I could use some help," he answered before the operator pulled the plug.

Edward and Padraig hadn't known they had a sister until after their mother died. Then, Charity started coming around the farm, asking James for money, and rides to various places, arguing with him as though she had known him for a long time.

James explained her presence to Edward and Padraig by saying that, years ago, when the widow was alone and pregnant, she was embarrassed by her situation, so he helped her out by allowing her to pretend he was the father of her child.

Actually, he had been riding their old nag Nellie, one scorching summer day when the horse was young and frisky. Feeling sorry for the sweating beast, he stopped at the creek to let her drink. He had ridden through the trees and into the water before noticing the widow-woman swimming in the deep shade. Clearly the woman wanted him or she wouldn't have jumped out of the water so undressed. Afterwards, she acted like everything that happened was a completely unwanted surprise.

How could a man on a horse be a surprise? Horses don't tiptoe around! She was dressed like a trollop, acted like a trollop, and she didn't stop him, because she didn't want him to stop. When she decided she was pregnant, it didn't mean he had anything to do with it. How could she think that he would believe that?

And besides, it didn't matter whose child Charity was, helping a pregnant widow-neighbor was a good thing to do. Being kind to a fatherless child couldn't hurt anyone. Especially after he no longer had a wife of his own to offend. Edward and Padraig didn't care why Charity was in their family; they loved her. She and the boys were good friends until the widow sold the farm and moved away.

Edward heard the widow died, but he didn't know what happened to Charity until she arrived in Newport one beautiful afternoon, on the back of Marie's older brother George's motorcycle. They were more than surprised to hear Charity was married to George. She proved it by slipping one arm out of her black leather jacket, to display a tattoo of a heart signifying the date of the event... on her shoulder.

After that, Marie tolerated their rare visits, but she was not fond of Charity. Her presence always preceded some craziness that left her feeling like she and Edward had been played for fools. Marie had learned to be vigilant when they arrived. Charity was a guest who came to your home empty-handed and left with something of yours.

She looked like a loose woman. Her clothes were tight, her fingernails were long, and she used a lot of perfume. Her hair was dyed blonde at a real beauty parlor, and she drank beer after dropping a shot glass full of whiskey in it, just like a man. When she had to work, she was a barmaid, and when she didn't work, she was a customer.

Charity didn't obey the ordinary standards of decorum that ruled their home. She slept until noon, even though her bed was their living room couch. Then she hung around the kitchen smoking cigarettes and drinking coffee. She paid no attention to her barely covered cleavage, even when it was the focus of everyone else. Complaining that she hated to get dressed because bras were uncomfortable, and gave her a rash when it was hot, she didn't wear one very often, even if it was cold.

This time Charity arrived without Uncle George. He had supposedly shipped out as an able-bodied seaman more than six months earlier, and hadn't been seen since. The captain of the ship he sailed on said he went ashore in Galveston and didn't return. Charity thought he had been thrown overboard after a card game (which he probably won, she said), or fell overboard while smoking (a reefer, Marie said).

Charity insisted that the circumstances surrounding George's disappearance had no doubt been altered to protect the company (Gulf Oil) from having to pay her a settlement. She tirelessly hounded the National Maritime Union to help her get "what she deserved," and was very involved in "developing a suit."

She said she had learned the value of suing when she slipped on a glob of spit at the dog track and sued the owners of the arena. No one was sure if she and George were really married, or had really sued, or what the results might have been. But Charity had been on crutches for a long time before declaring that they had finally reached a settlement.

Marie said, "If there was any spit, it came from George's mouth, and if Charity slipped in it, she did it on purpose after George pointed out the spot."

Edward called George the biggest liar he had ever met. And Marie responded that George was not wild until he met Charity. And it wasn't until *after* hanging around her, and some of her "convent" friends, he started acting like a crook. Almost.

Edward shouted, "What do you mean, *almost*? Your brother is a card-carrying *jailbird!*"

Marie called Charity a Jezebel, and a Mary Magdalene, and said the Sisters of Guadelupe "business" school she told Edward she attended was really a home for wayward girls in upstate New York.

Colleen listened intently while pretending not to hear. She was enthralled by the information in the air, but she knew that to respond as though she was alert to adult subjects would be the end of her presence. Acting small and bored, instead of spellbound and enraptured, she stared blankly at a schoolbook.

She remembered the picture Uncle George carried in his wallet. She and Sheila were with their parents one day when they took George and Charity for a ride around Ocean Drive while their motorcycle was getting fixed. George asked Edward to stop in front of a huge mansion with magnificent wrought iron gates which were standing ajar. He pulled Charity along and positioned her just inside the gates with the mansion in the distance behind her. Then he put his arm around her and handed Edward his camera. It was a nice camera, one that he'd found at a bar where he had lunch a few days earlier. The picture Edward took was a beauty. George often brought it out to show people where he lived. He never waited for someone to ask, because no one ever did.

George would show the snapshot to someone sitting next to him at a bar and say, "If you don't believe this is my house, ask my brother-in-law over there. He took the picture."

In the photo, Charity was wearing her fanciest outfit, the unborn-calf-skin suit that George brought back from Argentina. It was skin-tight, and the brown and white spotted leather did not stretch nearly as far as it should have to cover all of Charity. She wore a low-cut beige sleeveless sweater under the jacket, which at first glance confused people, because it appeared to be the color of her flesh.

No one in America had ever seen anything like that unborn-calf-skin suit, according to George. Marie said she was sure that was true. Colleen recognized her mother's expression; it looked like she had been sucking lemons. Repulsed by the hair on the soft spotted hide, the idea of unborn calves becoming clothing made Colleen queasy. Still, she had to admit, *no* one had ever seen anything like it.

When they were alone, Marie made Edward vow never to buy her anything made of unborn-calf-skin. After promising, Edward muttered, "Charity better be careful not to bend over in that outfit during hunting season."

Charity expected to receive a settlement from George's death at any time. She started almost every sentence with, "When I get my lump-sum payment." It was amazing how much attention she got with those seven words. One day she said, "When I get my lump-sum payment, Edward, do you think we should go into the lobstering business together?"

Edward was thrown off guard. "What do you mean?"

"Well, I think I should invest in something that makes money for me. You know, something that will support me. If I bought a lobster boat and you ran it, we would both make money. You could sell the lobsters and send me money every week. We would be doing something together that we couldn't do alone, and we could both make a living. What do you think?"

Edward was stunned. His sister! Or someone who might be partly his sister! His fabulous, beautiful, generous, wonderful, best, almost-sister in the world, who loved him and wanted to invest her lump-sum payment in him! He was so moved his heart rolled over in his chest; he actually felt it. Still, he knew enough to hold himself back when things seemed too good to be true.

"How would we find a boat to buy?" Charity asked.

Holding his breath, he answered slowly, "We would get the newspapers from New Bedford, and Bar Harbor, and Boston. And we would check the classified ads.

"I'd like a boat from someone who lobstered like I want to, someone who worked alone or with a single helper. Someone who has taken good care of his things and is retiring or has gotten sick and wants to quit," he said. "And I wouldn't buy a boat from a widow or a boat found adrift after a storm. And I wouldn't buy traps from someone who has a yard full of gear, but the boat and fisherman are missing.

"Things can be cheap, and you know how I like to squeeze a penny, but those situations are bad luck, and I know better than to try to change bad luck from the sea. Sometimes the bad luck doesn't follow the people, it stays with their things. Your destiny is your destiny."

Soon Edward and Charity were pouring over the classified "Boats for Sale" columns. They found two of interest. One was in Maine and the other in New Bedford. Charity wanted to get on her motorcycle and go to look at them, but Edward refused. He said his rear-end couldn't take it.

They went together in the family car, with Charity complaining the whole time. Edward no longer transported barrels of dead fish in the old Plymouth, but the smell was as ripe as last week's garbage. Sea gulls rested on the roof of that car when they got tired of flying. The back doors were tied shut with rope, and the car lumbered along slower than a turtle, according to Charity who was used to speed.

Edward had screwed a bench into the back seat area, and if the windows were open, the smell of fish was not a problem. However, they had to roll the windows up quickly when they stopped; otherwise, there was no predicting how many cats would be unwilling to leave when they returned.

Unfortunately, it was cold in Maine and they needed to drive with the windows shut and the heat turned on, a circumstance they referred to as "The Double No-No."

Charity had never spent as much time with Edward as she did on their trip to Maine to find a lobster boat. She discovered it was entirely too much. If she hadn't been able to talk him into wetting his whistle at several bars along the way, she would have abandoned the whole project.

When they finally got to Spruce Head, Maine, they found what Edward wanted. It was a thirty-two-foot wood hull, with a small house and a single motor for $2,500. It was a good price if you had money.

Charity negotiated with the lobsterman as though her purse was full of hundred-dollar bills. Edward stayed silent. Then she said, "Why don't you bring the boat down to New Bedford on Saturday and we'll pick it up there? Meanwhile, I'll give you a check for a deposit, and I'll bring the rest when we pick up the boat."

She whipped out a checkbook and wrote the man a check for $100.

"I'm getting a lump-sum settlement for my husband's death. and it is being transferred into my account today. Just in case there is a hold up because of paperwork, please don't cash the check until Saturday."

"I'll need cash when you take the boat," the man said.

"Of course," Charity reassured him.

Edward was almost dancing a jig. It wasn't until they stopped for beer again that he asked, "When did you find out about that lump-sum payment?"

Charity looked at him with astonishment. "What are you talking about? I have no idea when or *if* I'll ever get a dime. For all I know, George is shacked up with a woman in Mexico."

Edward groaned and dropped his head into his hands. His happiness fell into a familiar deep pit.

"I thought you wanted the boat," she said.

"I do. I want it a lot," he hissed.

"Then shut up and think about what to do on Saturday."

"There's nothing to do," he said. "Without money, he's not going to leave the boat, and if he cashes that check, we'll go to jail."

"Shut up," she said. "You're no help. I'll figure it out myself."

Edward was silent. His stomach was upset and he needed to stop to buy Maalox. Charity was quiet too.

Just before they arrived at home, Charity said, "I can figure this out, Edward, and we can pick up the boat on Saturday, if you keep your mouth shut. But if you tell Marie about this little problem as soon as we walk in the door, she will get herself all involved in my finances, and I'll be so busy explaining things to her, I won't be able to fix them."

"What do you expect me to do, lie to her?" he asked.

"No, definitely not. Just do nothing, and say nothing. Give me until Saturday. You won't need to say anything after that; and you will have saved Marie from worrying unnecessarily."

Charity was convincing, and Edward wanted to believe. He wouldn't consider making Marie worry for no reason, and he didn't want to worry either. Charity's problem involved a check and paperwork. That alone made it completely beyond him.

He was relieved to hear that she could solve it by herself. Thank God for the Poor Virgins of Guadalupe Convent School that George said had trained her in business skills.

On Wednesday when they were drinking at The Lobster Claw, Edward overheard Charity call her bank to see if a lump-sum payment had been deposited in her account. She re-checked the name of the woman she spoke to, and chatted with her about her missing husband and the cruel insensitivity she experienced when dealing with Gulf Oil. Then she called the head of the accounting department at Gulf Oil, Headquarters, person to person, collect, regarding a lump-sum settlement check for the death of her husband, a Gulf Oil employee. The check hadn't arrived at her bank as promised, and she needed to speak to someone who could find out where it was. The receptionist at Gulf Oil said that the head of the department was named Mr. Whirman, but he was on vacation. When the operator asked for his assistant, she was told that Mr. Morgenstein was sick.

Charity asked for the spelling of each name, the number of each extension, and wrote it all down. Finally, Mr. Peterson who was covering for Mr. Whirman, accepted the call. Charity explained that she had not received the check that Mr. Whirman told her was on its way. Obviously, it was either lost in the mail, or had not been sent at all. She wanted to know the name of the person who was in charge of issuing death benefit checks, and whether or not that person had sent one to her. She wrote down every person's name and extension number as her call was redirected. Then she rejoined Edward at the bar and ordered another beer.

"How is it going?" he wanted to know.

"Making progress," she answered.

Edward was overjoyed.

At home when he suggested they plan to pick the boat up on Saturday, Marie disdainfully said, "I'm from Missouri. I'll believe it when I see it."

Colleen was embarrassed by her mother's rude words. She wanted to apologize to her aunt, but she was not supposed to understand what was going on. She gathered flowers from a neighbor's yard and gave them to Charity. Her aunt lifted up her hair near her ear and kissed her neck while saying a "Mmmmm good," on her skin.

Her mother made a "Hmpph" sound and said, "Where are my flowers? I'm the one who puts food on this table."

"You mean leftovers from the big black purse?" Edward said as he pretended to run to kiss Marie. But she pushed him aside and left the room.

Meanwhile, Saturday approached.

Colleen wanted to ride back home in the new boat with her father and Charity. Marie begrudgingly agreed to go with her family to New Bedford, to pick up the boat, and drive the car home alone.

On Friday night Charity said she was going to a card game in the back room of The Acorn Bar and asked Edward if he wanted to come.

"I don't have that kind of money, but I'll walk over there and have a few beers with you," he offered.

Edward had been down at the wharf and one of his old friends had given him a big bluefish. It wasn't their favorite, but Marie cooked it, mashed it up with chopped onion and celery, put it in a pie crust and topped it with mashed potatoes left over from the school lunch. Edward took a look and said, "What is it?" Then he took a bite and said, "Shouldn't we put something on it?"

Charity got up and brought the ketchup bottle to the table saying, "You'll like it better now."

"Right," he said, after tasting it.

She always knew what he wanted.

They left after dinner to play cards. Marie looked at Colleen as the door closed behind them.

"She is either going to play cards until she loses the money for the boat, or she doesn't have any money, and she's planning to win enough to buy one," she announced.

Colleen was irate. "You say the worst, think the worst, and expect the worst. I wish I could go to New York and live with her."

"Believe me, I wish you would. All of you!" Her eyes full of tears, Marie returned to her knitting.

A subdued Edward drove his family to New Bedford. He had been out late, and didn't feel well. Charity sat in front with him, carrying a manila envelope that he assumed was full of cash. Last night she hadn't wanted to go home when he did, so he left her in the back room of The Acorn with a large roll of bills held together by a rubber band, resting beside her boilermaker.

Naturally, when they went to pick up the boat, she was wearing her finest outfit, the unborn-calf-skin suit, with the beige low-cut sweater that made men walk into door jambs. Colleen and her mother sat on the hard wooden bench in the back seat area that was favored by cats.

Marie had brought a thermos of coffee, a bag of fish-salad sandwiches and a dozen school-lunch brownies. She imagined an impromptu party on the boat after they signed over the title, and she had brought enough to share. Combining festivities, she hoped to celebrate the fisherman's retirement, Charity's boat purchase, and Edward's employment all at once. Marie was full of hope.

When they arrived and saw the boat and the fisherman already at the wharf, Edward was jittery with excitement. Charity navigated herself down the short ladder onto the deck and said, "Let's go for a quick spin around the harbor so that my brother can get the feel of her." She pressed the manila envelope to her bosom.

The fisherman stood with Edward in the small wheelhouse and revved her up. His wife sat on the back with Marie, Colleen, and Charity. At the end of the ride, the fisherman came over to Charity and took her check out of his wallet.

"I guess I can cash this now," he said.

Charity looked at him as though seeing him for the first time. "I wouldn't do that if l were you," she said.

The fisherman's smile froze. "You are a joker, aren't you?" He turned to Edward. "She's a joker... isn't she?"

"Not usually," Edward said softly. He looked like a balloon that had just been accidentally popped. At any moment Colleen expected to see him rise up squealing and flying in circles. Everyone was silent; it began to seem like this might not be a joke.

Charity said, "There's nothing to get in an uproar about. Come over here and look at this." She went into the wheelhouse and spilled the contents of the manila envelope onto the small counter. Several paper-clipped pieces of paper with names and telephone numbers on them fluttered out. Picking one up she read, "Mr. Whirman, 212-667-3876. See his title?" she asked. "Head of Accounting, Gulf Oil Headquarters."

The fisherman roared, "Who cares about his title? What do you think this is? Where's my money? I hope you don't think I'm going to call Mr. Whirman for it."

"Of course not. But I want you to know that I am serious, and the money is real. Edward was with me when I made all these phone calls to find out why it wasn't in my account yet."

Charity shook the papers in the air. "I'm just a poor widow fighting Gulf Oil. I'm sorry you might have to wait a few more days for your money. But I'm doing the best I can! Tell them, Edward!"

She pulled a tissue from between her breasts and the fragrance of Shalimar filled the air to a radius of about twelve feet.

Colleen had never seen Charity cry. With her make-up mask of indifference gone, she became a wrinkled, dappled mess.

The red-faced fisherman lurched toward Edward. "What do you know about this?"

"I don't know anything. I heard her making those phone calls, but I came here today thinking she had the money." Edward was miserable.

Marie was shaking, and Colleen was mortified.

Charity dabbed her eyes and looked into a tiny mirror. Tossing her hair back, she became herself again and said, "Look, I'll probably have the entire amount by next Saturday. Why waste all our preparations? We are ready to take the boat. You are ready to sell it. I have a hundred dollars cash. She deftly removed five warm twenties from a remote spot in the perfumed chasm between her powdered breasts and held them out to the fisherman.

"I will give you *this* now and the rest as soon as I receive it. In the meantime, my brother will use the boat to lobster and he will send you half of what he makes every week. That way he'll be paying for the boat, and you'll be receiving money on a regular basis until you get the total. We can finalize our whole agreement right now.

"If I get my money right away, as I expect I will, I'll pay you the balance immediately. My brother will then send *me* the payments. He *needs* to work to support *his* family. You don't want to be responsible for preventing *this* family from making it, do you?"

The fisherman said, "You people are a bunch of flim-flam gypsy con-artists! I'm not getting on a bus to Spruce Head Bay, Maine, with a hundred dollars in my pocket after leaving my boat with the likes of you!"

"Just a minute, Gus..."

They all turned as his wife spoke. "It's time for you to retire. You know what the doctor said. What difference does it *really* make if the money comes all at once or a little every week? Let's write something down so that we can go to the police if we don't get paid, and let's go home. We have already had more trouble than we can handle."

She reached over, took the five twenties from Charity, and gave them to her husband. Addressing him again, she said, "Look at the kid. She's scared to death. And look at *his* poor wife. She can't stop shaking. They're not part of any flim-flam gypsy family.

"And this poor man. All he wants to do is catch lobsters. Remember when you were like that? Out in all kinds of bad weather... he's not trying to steal a boat. He's the one who will send the money.

"We don't have to worry about Gulf Oil, or this city woman. They would never care about us anyway. But this man is a seaman like you. He won't cheat us, and we should trust him."

Suddenly, the gulls stopped cawing and the air was still. In the profound silence, Gus took a pipe from his plaid flannel pocket with a jittery hand.

Reluctantly he replied, "Okay." Then he added, "But the first time I don't get a payment, I'm going to the police."

They wrote everything down on the manila envelope and each of them signed it before giving the envelope to the fisherman. Afterwards, Marie passed out sandwiches and brownies and coffee. Charity took a small leather box from her purse. It contained a flask and four small metal cups. She poured shots for the fisherman and Edward before taking one herself. "Hair of the dog," she said and drank.

Gus and his wife accepted a ride to the bus station from Marie, and Colleen decided to drive home with her mother. She curled up in the big front seat of the car and slept most of the way home, while Marie played the radio and sang along. It was almost like the old days, when Sheila was there.

If the day had even remotely resembled the one he had imagined, Edward would have been elated to be on his own boat triumphantly steaming from New Bedford into Newport harbor. As it was, he was on edge, wound tight, a bundle of nerves ready to spring out of control. Ordinarily he mulled things over slowly, and after a few beers he put them in order for his mind to review.

On this day, there had been no time to figure out exactly what had happened, or how the parts of it interacted. He had never experienced so many cockamamie circumstances and emotions in such a short time. No matter how careful he was, or how hard he tried to avoid his sister's confusion, here he was, mixed up with her again.

"Crap!" he muttered. "It's always a problem when men are not in charge."

The women, specifically Charity and the fisherman's wife, had usurped the men's power and made decisions and arrangements they would all have to live with now. Who knew how it had happened? After he figured it out, he would discuss it with Skinhead and Marie to get their take on it. Then he would analyze his thoughts and develop his own opinion of the whole bag of worms. A lot had happened and he was left holding the bag. He didn't want to talk to Charity about it until he had absorbed all aspects of the boat deal that he was now bound by.

But Charity could not wait for him to understand. She was so jubilant she wanted to laugh and hoot and make merry... immediately. "What a great deal," she crowed. "Aren't you thrilled?" She had the flask out again, and poured another shot for each of them.

He chugged the whiskey and looked at her. "Why?"

"Well, for one thing you have a boat, and it hasn't cost you anything yet. For another thing, you're going to make a ton of money."

He began to see her clearly. He said, "How? By lobstering? You are sooooo nuts!"

"What's wrong?" she wondered.

"How much do you think I will be able to sell my lobsters for?"

She said, "I don't know, five dollars a pound?"

"More like one dollar a pound," he answered.

"Oh. I thought they were *real* expensive," she said.

"They are, if you go to a restaurant and buy one for dinner. But I sell to a wholesaler. That's different. And now I have to buy gear, and pay Gus, and buy bait, and fuel, and get a license, all before I feed my family."

"And pay me," Charity added.

"How?" Edward asked. "And why? It looks like I only owe you a hundred dollars."

"I'm talking about the money you'll owe me after my lump-sum settlement pays off the boat."

Edward's eyes bored right through Charity. He turned the motor off and put the ignition key in his pocket.

"Why are we stopping, Edward? What's wrong?" she cried as they rocked in very heavy swells. Charity was scared. She had heard that sometimes as a child Edward held his breath until he passed out when he didn't get his way. She had never experienced this side of him.

"I'm not going home," Edward said. "I don't want to. In fact, I don't care if I never arrive in Newport. I might as well throw the key away." He pulled his hand out of his pocket and threw something. There was a splash.

Charity's stomach turned over. "Edward!" she screamed. "Please tell me that wasn't the key. Did you throw the key away? Tell me, what do you want?"

"I never want you to mention that damned lump-sum settlement to me again. I am going to get a hundred dollars and pay you back tomorrow. And as soon as I do, I want you to put your rear-end on that motorcycle, and head toward New York. And you'd better swear to God," he ordered.

Charity held her right hand straight up. "I swear to God," she promised.

Edward took the key out of his pocket and restarted the engine.

Charity never did get a lump-sum settlement from Gulf Oil. It was just as well, because George reappeared a few months later. He said he had been an undercover agent for the government, helping to capture the leaders of a Mexican drug gang. After an initial period of hostility, Charity welcomed him with open arms and proudly wore the ten-carat, semi-precious, topaz ring he brought home for her.

Edward told Marie that someone at The Acorn had heard at the union hall in Providence that George had been caught selling drugs and was imprisoned in a Mexican jail. He used the picture of his "mansion" to convince a guard that he was rich, and he persuaded the poor fellow to help him escape.

George's family was supposed to pay a ransom for his safe return. No one ever knew if that story was true, but Edward noticed that George never shipped out on a tanker bound for Texas again.

Since Edward was a man who didn't believe in banks, Marie was stuck with the boat payments. When the weather was too severe for small craft fishermen, or lobsters were scarce, or Edward was too drunk to fish, Marie was forced to make the boat payments herself. On those occasions she took their meager cash to the post office and bought a money order she purposely made out to Gus's wife. It took five years to pay off the boat. They couldn't own a house because of those payments. And whenever Marie heard the sound of a motorcycle, she pursed her lips and looked around for Charity.

8 COLLEEN

Colleen's parents looked at her like she had grown a second head when she announced that a local college was out of the question; she was only in eighth grade, and she wanted to go to school far away. After witnessing years of her mother's disappointments and her father's failures, she had distanced herself from both, and she wanted to get away, far away. In addition, she notified her parents that she needed braces. Instead of letting the matter rest, Colleen made an appointment with a classmate's orthodontist and brought a proposal home that involved a monthly payment.

Marie was astounded. It hadn't been that long since Edward had talked Marie into having all her teeth pulled because fillings were a recurring expense, and false teeth were cheaper if you bought the whole set at once. "After all, you're going to need them someday," he assured her. It was true... a lot of people they knew already did.

Her parents had never heard of anyone having braces. They thought it was a foolish idea. Still, her mother didn't want to say no to Colleen. She wanted the child to realize that she should not ask for expensive things.

"Your expectations are beyond our means. You're asking for college and braces. You can't have everything you want." She said, "Life is full of choices."

She might have said it with patience, and love, and the hope that this strange child of hers would come to her senses soon. Or maybe she didn't. Whichever way it was said, Colleen took this conversation to mean that she would have to select between braces or college. It was a bold suggestion, and a big decision.

Marie was hopeful. "She'll forget about it by dinnertime," she told Edward.

It didn't take long for Colleen to decide. She announced, "I choose college because it is more important for my future."

Marie and Edward looked at her blankly. "What is she talking about?" they asked themselves. But the future wasn't a topic they visited, and her expectations weren't mentioned again... until she needed a parental signature on her course selection form.

"Why would you take Latin and French and Algebra?" Marie wondered.

"I need those for college."

Edward turned from John Cameron Swayze and the evening news. "Who is going to send you?"

"You said you would."

"What have you ever done for me?" He turned back to the news.

"Don't you care about my future? What do you expect me to do after high school?"

"Get a job. Start paying room and board, learn to cook like your mother so someone will hopefully marry you and take you off our hands."

Marie erased the selections and substituted typing and bookkeeping before signing the form.

The next day at school Colleen said that she had lost the form. She filled out a new one and signed Marie's name. There was no further discussion until senior year when her guidance counselor met with her to see where she planned to attend college.

"I don't know. I don't have any money," Colleen replied.

"Then I guess you're not going."

"What about a scholarship?" she asked.

"You still need money. Every application requires a check, a graduation picture, letters of recommendation, and transcripts. And most scholarships cover only a small part of the total cost."

Colleen didn't apply. She blamed her parents for lying to her when they told her to choose. Truth be told, they didn't remember any of it. Colleen thought she was stuck in Newport, but someone told her that hospital nursing schools were really cheap. The three-hundred-dollar check Aunt Charity said she was going to give her as a graduation gift would cover the total tuition for three years.

"If it doesn't bounce," Marie reminded her.

Hospital schools included room and board; some even offered a stipend. Colleen would finally move away, and she was elated. After graduation from a nursing program, she planned to get a scholarship to Boston University, study English, and earn a degree after one year. Between the low cost of nursing and the college scholarship (absolutely no problem), she would graduate at the same time as the rest of her contemporaries. She applied to three nursing schools with tuition of less than four hundred dollars. In each of her interviews she was asked why she wanted to be a nurse.

"I want to get away from home, and I don't have the money to go away to college," Colleen responded.

The Director of Admissions at Worchester City Hospital School of Nursing peered over her glasses. "Have you applied anywhere else?"

"Yes," Colleen replied.

"Were you accepted?"

"No."

"Your transcript and your SATs are outstanding. Do you have any idea why not?"

"No," Colleen responded.

"Has anyone else asked you why you wanted to be a nurse?"

"Yes." Colleen nodded.

"I suppose you gave them the same answer you gave me?" the Director wondered.

"Yes... it's the truth."

"But it will not get you accepted anywhere. In fact, you won't get a chance to be a dog-nurse with that response."

Colleen was dumbfounded.

The Director continued, "I'm going to take a chance on you. Don't disappoint me by quitting."

At the end of their first year in school, nine months of classes and three months on the wards, trainees were scheduled to attend an autopsy. Everyone was apprehensive, Colleen more than most. On the appointed day, they were divided into groups and assigned to an instructor.

When the first group returned from the morgue, they twittered with gruesome details. Colleen listened as one of her classmates complained that she would never eat lemon meringue pie again, after watching the pathologist cut into an obese man's quivering, yellow belly fat. The room was too small, the girl added, and the students crowded around the steel table trying not to inhale. She said she had to vomit.

Colleen had heard enough. Before her group assembled, she told the instructor that she was assigned to a different group. When the day was over, each instructor thought she had attended with the other group. Instead of being relieved, Colleen felt guilty. She expected to be found out at any moment. Her dishonesty had been impulsive. Now she feared what would happen when it was discovered.

She imagined herself forced to attend an autopsy without a group of taller girls to stand behind, unable to camouflage her averted eyes. The Chief Pathologist, Dr. D for "Dracula," would probably want to teach her a lesson by selecting a particularly horrible dissection for her to watch. Colleen was a wreck contemplating the possibilities; she imagined herself accidentally left alone with the cadaver while Dracula left to find a sharper saw.

Knowing that her own deceit put her in this position made it worse. Working on the wards had taken a toll; the students were on each other's nerves. The few who initially believed that a handsome young doctor was waiting in the next treatment room with a glass slipper, no longer believed fairy tales. Working on the wards was a sure cure for romantic fantasy.

Real patients were usually old, and disgusting and sick. One ancient diabetic, whose ulcerated legs were bandaged with wax paper, had been found unconscious in an abandoned building. Open sores were visible in opaque crinkles while blood and puss oozed through ragged seams and layers. As his admission nurse, Colleen had to clean him. When she soaked the wax paper from his wounds, he screamed, "What is that on my leg? It's your lipstick! What are you doing to me with your mouth, you harlot!"

The man was restrained, legs and arms. After he was cleaned, the doctor debrided the necrotic parts of his only foot at the bedside with Colleen assisting, as instructed. When black skin and tissue was cut, the man had no reaction at all. But as surgical tools invaded the pink flesh of his raw wound, and clunked against a flash of white bone, his cries became harrowing.

The doctor did not raise his voice to communicate with Colleen, nor did he look up. He waited until the man took a breath, and muttered, "Which is worse for a homeless derelict? Getting drunk and freezing to death in a vacant building? Or having your remaining foot amputated?"

The crazed man heard the word "amputated" and wrestled one arm out of its restraint to grab a bottle of alcohol from the bedside table.

"Aiiieeeeyhh! This butcher is cutting my foot off!"

He threw the bottle at the doctor, causing the scalpel to slice deeply into his own lower leg. A pulsing gusher spewed blood.

"It's the anterior tibial. I've got it here. You apply pressure on the femoral artery," the doctor calmly ordered. Colleen fumbled with the sheet and the Johnny.

The old man screamed louder. "This harlot is sucking blood from my stump! Oooweeeeghh!"

The noise brought the student-nurse-instructor who stepped in front of Colleen and took over. "Get him back in that restraint," she said over her shoulder in a calm, quiet voice.

For the first time since the crisis, Colleen had a moment to look at the old man. He had his fist in his mouth and was chewing on it between screams. When she pulled it free to reattach the restraint, his volume increased to emergency-siren level. After quickly tightening the other restraints, she picked up the bloody linen that had been thrown on the floor.

It had been a terrible day; she had seen and heard too much. Her uniform was filthy and she could feel sweat running down the sides of her face and the small of her back. Luckily, her shift was almost over. In the bathroom, she splashed cold water on her face and randomly pinned her hair back.

Desperate days like this one, and horrific procedures like the debridement, needed time and space to assimilate. It was necessary to recuperate. However, that summer on the wards there was no time between crises.

Her patient the next morning was a nineteen-year-old boy who had shot himself in the head in a failed suicide attempt. Because his specialized care required a nurse's full attention, the students were assigned to spend a whole eight-hour shift with him in rotation; it gave the floor nurses a break. Due to a systemic infection, he was in complete isolation. His mother sat on a straight chair outside the doorway and watched for hours. The boy's tracheotomy was continually clogged with bubbles of viscous green phlegm that made him struggle for air, and his oxygen tent didn't seem to help; rather, it got in the way. There was no air-conditioning in the hospital and the temperature inside the plastic tent where the patient's bed was located was equivalent to the Sahara Desert in Worchester, Mass.

In a coma and non-responsive to pain, most of the time the boy's eyes were unfocused. Tears fell relentlessly to his hairline and around his ears to the pillow. As Colleen suctioned his trachea tube, he made sounds that could only be compared to a mortally wounded animal.

A glance at the chart attached to his bed revealed, in detail, his nurse's notes that documented every aspect of his care and condition, including his many long-lasting erections. She added her observations of tears, phlegm color, clogged breathing tube, and changes under the sheets when indicated. It was all she could do. She didn't want to embarrass either of them by looking underneath the covers.

Before it was her turn to care for him again, his room was empty. News of his death spread through the freshman class like a healing breeze.

Some patients' demands for constant attention were just plain annoying. The bathroom occupied many of them, all day long. If they hadn't had a bowel movement or couldn't pee, they acted like it was a major catastrophe instead of a mini vacation for an overworked colon or bladder. When Colleen was assigned to cardiac patients on complete bed rest, her instructors expected her to do everything but breathe for them. One obese man looked at the basin and soap she placed in front of him as though he wondered what it was for. There were five others assigned to Colleen that morning and she didn't have time to clean them all. Someone would just have to wash his own face.

She pulled the curtains around the beds of her other patients while pondering how to get enough leverage to change the sheets under the obese one. She decided to start with the easy patients, but by lunchtime she still hadn't finished with them, and the obese man had died. The charge nurse was horrified. At first she thought the man had over exerted himself while taking a sponge bath. She looked at Colleen and hissed, "What is wrong with you? He *can't* wash himself."

She didn't say, "Murderer," but the word hung in unspoken fury in the cubicle until she moved the soap dish, face cloth, and towel and noticed they were dry. In fact, Colleen hadn't even had time to put water in the basin. "Thank God," the supervisor said with relief. The man had died waiting for a nurse with hot water.

Colleen was not relieved. She was aghast as she surveyed the mound of clammy flesh before her, still waiting to be washed. The old nurse remembered her own days as a trainee as she observed an overwhelmed Colleen blowing her nose and wiping her eyes. When her first patient died, she cried too. When she was young and sympathetic, she cried a lot.

Actually, Colleen was covering her nose with a tissue before breathing. It didn't help. The atmosphere in the small partition became more and more unpleasant. Then he farted.

"Not flatulence too," the supervisor remarked.

An odor, fouler than any Colleen had ever smelled, emanated from the dead man. She was afraid that raising the sheet would release more of it. Bathing anything that smelled like that was out of the question. She looked for a window to throw herself from, as a wave of nausea rolled up through her digestive tract toward her throat.

Attempting to distract herself from the reverse peristalsis in her gut, she wondered...

If the fat man's large sphincter had relaxed, and the bed was full and fetid, how long had it been since he died? They had just studied postmortem activity. Colleen tried to concentrate on the timeline for loss of involuntary muscle tone after death. Ordinarily, she could rattle off statistics like a bookie handicapping a race. Not today.

She thought of the sphincter closest to the esophagus, the lower esophageal sphincter, the peristalsis, the journey through the duodenum, jejunum, and ileum, to the colon to the anus. Muscle tone... what was the sequence involved there? How long did it take a low-sodium breakfast to exit the body involuntarily, and smell up the ward like cow dung at an abattoir? Up to thirty-six hours? Not today.

And what about the digestive state of her breakfast? It was rising into her throat and threatened to project itself across the man, onto the white curtain like a droopy Rorschach stain of bacon and eggs, with ketchup and raisin toast garnish. What if it couldn't stay airborne as far as the curtain? How long before she blew vomit all over the dead man's face and it was just another thing to wash? She put her hand up to her mouth, hoping to hold it closed, but she could not. Her supervisor tossed the emesis basin to her in time for the second wave.

The senior nurse instructor said, "You seem upset. Would you like to go back to the residence to change and compose yourself?"

Colleen was more than relieved. "Yes, I'd appreciate that."

An escape from the small enclosure containing this glabrous slab of dead flesh had been on her mind since she entered.

"You go. I'll take care of preparations here," the nurse announced.

Colleen took the elevator to the ground level and waited at the light to cross the street to the nurse's residence.

"Colleen! Colleen!"

She looked around. There on her motorcycle was Aunt Charity in black leather with Uncle George behind her. The man on George's Harley was a stranger. They glided to the curb. "Wow! You look like something the cat dragged in. What happened?"

"It was a tough day."

"Meet Joe!" Charity said. "He was on George's ship and when he told us he lived in Worchester, we decided to give him a ride home, and come to see you at the same time."

Colleen replied, "I've been sent back to my room to clean up, but by the time I take a shower and change, my shift will be over. I'm free after that. Can you wait?"

"We'll drop Joe off at his place and be back in an hour. You can bring a friend if you want. We'll take you both out for dinner."

They thundered off with Colleen wondering how to avoid telling them that she was miserable. After all, they paid for this education she was beginning to hate.

In her room, she took her clothes off. A long shower helped. Afterwards, she even washed her shoes. When Colleen turned her radio on, one of her favorite songs was playing, and she hummed along. Barbra Streisand's words entered Colleen's mind like a message, a suggestion. She was never going to save the world one bedpan at a time. If she stayed in nurse's training she would get a job as a nurse, and her degree, when she finally got it, would be in nursing. Her education would commit her to a career she didn't want, and would never want, a career full of disgusting sounds and smells and procedures. It was time to make a change.

Making just one someone happy, would make Colleen happy too. She was sure of it. After a while she would get married and have children and make them happy. In the meantime, she would make herself happy... by leaving this school of bloody horrors. With a full orchestra playing, making someone happy seemed entirely possible.

Her friend Beverly followed the music into her room. "My family is moving to Florida. I'm going to quit school and go with them."

"Wow. Congratulations," Colleen said.

"College is cheap there, and I'm going to apply. Why don't you apply too? We can be roommates."

"Maybe I will. Meanwhile, my crazy Aunt Charity and Uncle George are in town. They want to take me out tonight. Would you like to come to a strange biker's bar, or motorcycle club, with my weird relatives?"

"If this is the Aunt Charity I've heard about, I wouldn't miss it for anything."

They went down to the foyer when Charity and George arrived wearing cowboy hats that George had acquired on one of his adventures. Her aunt and uncle looked like they had just left a Hell's Angels convention and were on their way to a rodeo. Under her black leather jacket, Charity wore the low-cut flesh-colored sweater that Colleen recognized from the unborn-calf-skin outfit.

Beverly, a tiny, flat-chested girl, was clearly fascinated by the opulent cleavage on display. Colleen sat behind Uncle George and Beverly sat behind Aunt Charity. They waved to the girls at the second-floor windows of the residence, and disappeared in a smoky whirlwind of reverberations and backfires while their classmates stared down in disbelief.

They stopped in front of Chez Francois, the fanciest restaurant in town, and used the reserved parking space next to the doorman for the motorcycles. Colleen was immediately nervous. She bent close to George's ear and whispered, "This place looks very expensive, and we don't have any money."

"Don't you worry, honey. It looks perfect for you. First class! Besides, this is my treat. Be sure you and Beverly only order soup."

When they were taken to their seats, Uncle George said something in French. The waiter looked at them strangely and hustled them to a different table. "Magnifique!" George said and clapped the man on the back.

Colleen was surprised. "I didn't know you spoke French."

"I was wrongly convicted of an immigration offense when I came to the assistance of a French-Canadian bootlegger. It took about six months to get it straightened out. In the meantime, I learned a little of the language."

"What did you say to our waiter?" Colleen wanted to know.

"You are too young to know," George replied. There was a moment of silence while they decided not to pry.

The waiter put her napkin in Colleen's lap before leaving to get Cokes for the girls and whiskey with beer chasers for George and Charity.

When they looked at the menu, the prices were outrageous. George said, "Let's start with soup. What do you like, Beverly?"

She ordered, "Creme de Petits Pois," and the rest of them followed with "Soupe l'Oignon, Vichyssoise, and Bisque De Cribiches." George spoke so loudly when ordering the Cribiches, Colleen wished she could disappear.

When the soup arrived, they passed their cups to each other for tasting. George and Charity ate with gusto. Then he called the waiter. "*Garçon*," he began. "This is too salty. Try it yourself."

"*Non, non, monsieur*," the waiter demurred. "I will get you another."

"Thank you, but I don't want another. It will ruin my dinner."

"That is fine," the waiter responded. "You will not be charged. Now, I will check on your entree."

"Wait, *garçon*," George continued. "The vichyssoise was not as cold as it should be. I'm afraid my wife will be sick."

The waiter's eyes opened wider. "Madame, I will get another vichyssoise for you."

"No, don't bother," Charity said. "I'm a little queasy, and I'm afraid to have any more. I think the cream was rancid."

"I will take both soups off the bill. Now I must check with the kitchen for your entrees."

"Wait, *garçon*," George said. "Our daughters don't know how *Les Potages* should taste. That's why they didn't complain. But my wife tasted them, didn't you dear?"

Charity surveyed the four empty bowls and said, "I tasted the *petits pois*. It had too heavy a flavor of nutmeg, and the *l'oignon* did not have Swiss cheese on it, I'm afraid."

"*Un moment.*" The waiter rushed to the kitchen and conferred with the chef. "The cheese used was *emmantaler*. It is the variety of Swiss cheese that our chef prefers. *Je le regret.*"

"That's too bad," Charity said. "If I had known you used *emmantaler*, I would not have let Colleen order it. I'm very careful about the cheese that she eats."

"Would *you* like to speak to the manager?" the waiter wondered, his eyes bugging out.

"Not necessarily. If you can correct the bill, we won't interrupt our dinner. If not, then of course I'll speak to *le manager*."

"I'll speak to him myself," the waiter said. After a quick conference, he was back. "Your entrees will be ready in one minute, and there is no charge for the soups. *Je le regret.*"

Colleen and Beverley had followed George's instructions and only ordered soup. They were used to eating like birds in restaurants to save money. Besides, Colleen was still overcome by her day in the wards, and Beverly was no bigger than a bird.

George and Charity had *chateaubriand* for two. When their dinner was served, mouth-watering delicacies covered the table. They placed a few carrots, potatoes, and pieces of beef on their bread plates and passed one to each girl, coaxing them to try everything.

"This is delicious," Colleen and Beverly agreed. George and Charity filled the bread plates again and passed them back to the girls. Then they divided the warm bread in the breadbasket, and when they finished the first loaf, they had another.

Everyone seemed to be enjoying dinner until George called, "*Garçon*," and explained, "this is too rare for me." The waiter took the meat to the kitchen. When it was returned, George pronounced it perfect. He served several slices to Charity. "Too well done," she declared.

"*Garçon*," she called.

He was right at her elbow. "I know," he answered. "Do you want the chef to cook another?"

"No. We don't have time to wait. And besides, we've had so many carrots and potatoes we aren't hungry anymore. *Je le regret.*"

The maître d' and George spoke French in an alcove. There was apparently some concern about the attention their party attracted that made the staff eager to get them out of the restaurant. Ultimately, George reported that the maître d' was pleased to receive half of the charge for *chateaubriand*, and the drinks, like the soup, were complimentary. They roared off to an ice cream stand for dessert.

Sitting on a picnic bench at the edge of dark, Colleen finished telling her Aunt Charity about the day. "The only way I can make it here is to change my heart."

"How?" Charity asked.

"I have to look at people as though they aren't hurting, bleeding, and scared. I have to think of them as diseases, nothing more. When

I leave for the day, I have to turn my back and walk away from their pain," Colleen answered.

"That's right," Beverly said. "Right now, we take them back to the residence in our minds, and it's torture. I'm glad my family is moving, and I'm glad I'm quitting."

Charity looked at Colleen. "And you're quitting too, aren't you?"

"Will you be terribly disappointed?" Colleen asked.

"Not for a minute. You don't see me doing something that I don't want to do. How could I expect it of you?"

"But the money you gave me to go to nursing school?"

"Oh well, they haven't gotten that much of the money. I talked them into a small partial payment to start. And they won't get another cent, will they George?"

"Nope."

"I feel so bad about wasting a year and disappointing everyone," Colleen continued.

George spoke up, "You know, kid, you haven't wasted a year. We saw your grades, and we know you learned a lot. Knowledge is something that can never be taken away. It will always be with you. No one is disappointed, and no one will ever be disappointed with someone who is true to herself."

They had finished their ice cream cones and climbed onto the back of the Harleys.

George and Charity invited both girls to return to Brooklyn with them and offered to show them a fun time in New York City. Colleen and Beverly ran up to their rooms, took a few sweatshirts and jeans and left.

The weekend was worth it. They saw their first Broadway play by sneaking into *Mame* during intermission, and they had lunch at the Carnegie Deli, leaving before the bill came. They went to Central Park and The Tavern on the Green, where George found a perfect table where the previous customers had barely touched their beers, and the waitstaff had taken the check but the table had not been bussed.

The girls each had almost a full mug, Charity and George ordered shots to accompany their leftover beers, and replenished the whiskey from Charity's little flask. On Sunday afternoon, George and Charity roared into Port Authority Terminal with the girls leaning into the turns like real bikers.

As soon as they were dropped off, there was a shooting in front of a bus near them. People screamed and ran. Colleen and Beverly bent low and rushed to board the bus marked Worchester. In the moments before they could take a deep breath, they giggled. The trip had been an unforgettable finale to their time at nursing school, enough excitement for a long time.

Her nursing experience made it easy for Colleen to get a job at the state mental hospital as an attendant. She sublet a couch in another girl's room, and began to save money in earnest. Soon she and Beverly were accepted at the University of Florida, Gainesville, for the January term. Colleen had enough money for one semester of tuition, books, and dorm. She moved into Grove Hall with Bev as her roommate, and found a job in a restaurant that provided baked potatoes and salads. With her tips, she bought breakfast. The rest of the day tended to take care of itself.

9 WILSON

Near the university a once imposing antebellum mansion had been haphazardly festooned with gingerbread balconies and hollow columns before being divided into efficiency apartments for students. Colleen passed it several times a week when she walked to and from Grove Hall, and her job making salads at The Steak Place.

One night a song drew her to the front steps. Mike Wilson from her French Lab was already seated, drinking a beer disguised by pouring it into an empty Coke can. He nodded and indicated the space beside him. Two young men with strong voices were playing guitars and singing "Sloop John B." Students spontaneously gathered in ones and twos, bringing beer, and sharing cigarettes that flashed bright then dimmed, like fireflies.

Students stopped to sing along, or listened to a few tunes on their way going out or coming back. New voices floated closer when disembodied singers left the shadows and walked past. Drinking, singing silhouettes lounged on the wide steps. Colleen sipped beer from a soda can that Wilson offered. The beauty of many voices united made her too emotional to join them. Then, as mysteriously as the hootenanny began, it was over. Musicians put instruments into their cases and people drifted away.

Colleen said, "That was fantastic. Does it happen often?"

"No. Only when I should be studying. Like now. Are you hungry?"

Colleen didn't answer at first. A fluttering thing had just happened in her heart. "Something wrong?" he asked.

"No, not at all," she answered.

"Are you hungry?"

"Yes, but I have dinner with me. A baked potato," she raised the small bag.

"Sounds great, but I'm in the mood for hot donuts, and I know where they're being made right now. Want one?"

"Sure." They went to his car. Colleen had no idea what existed just a few blocks from campus. Wilson bought half a dozen hot, glazed Krispy Kremes, and they each ate one before she turned to say something to him while licking warm donut glaze, and he surprised her with a sugary kiss. He started the motor and drove to Grove, where they talked and finished the donuts.

After what seemed like a few minutes, he said, "Well, I'd better get going. It's getting late."

Colleen's curfew in the dorm was eleven p.m., and she had no idea where the time had gone. It was two in the morning, and she would be in trouble if she couldn't crawl in through Bev's ground-floor window.

Wilson was multi-lingual, raised in Spain, and had gone to a boarding school. To most people he was a freckle-faced red-head; to Colleen he was a young Cary Grant, who played Edith Piaf records, growled near her ear, and whispered in French.

They had donuts together almost every night... for about a week. The time they spent together became the highlight of her day, until the night he said, "I want you," after an amazing amount of sugar kissing, and she had no idea what to say. Her silence continued as he started the car and brought her back to the dorm. He didn't call again.

Colleen stopped going to French class, and only showed up for work. She slept late and went to bed the minute she came back to her room. After a few days of moping, Beverly insisted that she go to a football game with a friend of her latest boyfriend. The idea of being fixed up was not appealing to Colleen, but she was too wilted to resist.

It was the first football game on campus that Beverly, a former high school cheerleader, attended. She was a ninety-eight-pound bundle of energy who bounced with excitement when she saw the spectacle of band and twirlers and the cheerleading squad that even included male gymnasts. Steve Spurrier, the quarterback, was expected to win the Heisman Trophy, and the standing-room-only crowd anticipated a dramatic win. They were not disappointed.

Colleen had seen her date around the Biology lab, a handsome pre-med student named Mark. Every day he wore a different starched buttoned-down short-sleeved shirt with fold lines that indicated it was either brand new, or had been professionally laundered and starched.

For Colleen, who wore a borrowed dress and hoped her date bought her a snack for dinner, the idea of getting clothes professionally laundered was the height of wasteful spending.

Mark had a ton of questions about nursing and her summer on the wards at Worchester. They were having a wonderful time until they were separated in the crush at the refreshment booth. Colleen moved to a spot in front of the stands, and waited to be found.

Straight ahead at the edge of the field she saw Wilson waiting for the game to resume. When he saw her, he raised his fancy camera and took her picture. Then he walked over and said, "Look at the crowd behind you. All the girls are wearing pastel colors. You are the only one wearing bright blue. You stand out." She had a sudden moment of dizziness.

"Colleen," she heard her name and turned toward the stands. Mark smiled and held their drinks high while gesturing toward their seats. Wilson was back on the sidelines taking pictures when Colleen looked next. She didn't feel much like watching a football game anymore, and when Beverly and the guys wanted to go to dinner after the game, she asked them to drop her off at the dorm. They were clearly annoyed.

One day Jualita, a casual friend on her floor, mentioned that she was dating a young Cuban orthodontist who worked as a janitor in their building while his USA certification was in process. According to Jualita he had excellent qualifications, and he moonlighted. Colleen hadn't seen an orthodontist since the seventh grade, but the possibility of a bargain appealed to her. She found Raoul looking out a second-floor window while he leaned against his mop. He invited her to sit on the top step and began his consultation. He said he'd had excellent success straightening teeth by pulling some of them to ease crowding, thereby allowing the remaining ones to fill in the spaces naturally and quickly. He suggested they begin with an appointment the next evening. They agreed to meet at the dental school where Raoul's custodial key opened a lab with a dental chair and equipment.

Raoul's father, a successful oral surgeon, had to leave his assets behind when politics made their family's escape from Havana imperative. Starting over was hard on all of them.

Young and handsome, Raoul's BMOC lifestyle had been interrupted by the war, and now financial sacrifice and hard work stood between him and the American dream. In Cuba, he had been a magnet for beautiful women, but in America he cleaned floors at a university full of gorgeous girls who looked right through him. He was diminished in stature, treated like a common janitor.

After fixing the light in Jualita's room, he fell in love with her because she wore hot pants so tight she needed to lie down in order to unzip the zipper, revealing her white cotton underpants labeled "Sunday"... at least that is the way Raoul imagined it.

To convince her to date him, he told her he was a new orthodontist forced to accept menial work while waiting for his paperwork to be verified. In his mind it was a simple exaggeration. After all, he observed a great deal during his janitorial shifts, and had listened to dental conversation all his life. He felt qualified to be an imposter, and his desire for Jualita required it. In reality, his studies in Cuba weren't transferable, because he didn't have acceptable grades. He couldn't pass proficiency exams, because he couldn't find someone to take them in his place.

His immigration paperwork had already been approved and his lowly job matched his qualifications. Fortunately, friends of his father arranged lodging in Gainesville, and the job at the university. If he passed remedial classes and applied for admission, he could attend school year-round on the trimester system and graduate in a few years at a cost his family could afford.

The whole plan depended on his initiative. That was the problem. Meanwhile, his fictional education as a dentist had not resulted in a date with Jualita, but he had pulled a fuse out of the electric box controlling her side of the hall. The resulting blackout gave him an opportunity to fiddle with the light in her room, and he hoped to be fiddling with her soon.

Jualita's effort to help him by sending him a patient named Colleen presented a dilemma. The last thing he wanted was a real patient. She was his first patient, and he knew as soon as she opened her mouth that she would also be his last. He pushed against her lower bicuspids; they seemed to be stuck in her gums by cement. "Strong teeth like rocks," he mumbled in Spanish, as he started to sweat. "I don't know how I got myself into this mess," he continued in Spanish.

Colleen didn't understand his words, but the tone alarmed her. Her frightened eyes unnerved him. Finally, he had an idea. "Let's start with an impression of your bite," Raoul said as he opened a plethora of tiny drawers looking for a form and plaster. Nauseous and dizzy, he hoped he didn't faint.

After filling the form and stuffing it in her mouth while she gagged, he said, "I need a break."

At that moment, the door rattled.

"What's going on in here?" One of the real dental professors had come back to retrieve something.

Raoul jumped away from Colleen.

"What are you doing to her?" The professor rushed to see.

A tense Raoul explained while she gurgled.

"I can't believe a nitwit janitor tells a student he is going to straighten her teeth and she arrives like a lab-rat for the experiment. A janitor! Just when you think you've seen it all." Dr. Martine wrestled with the tin form of congealed goop in Colleen's mouth.

"Young lady, Raoul is going to visit security with me right now. I will see you in my office tomorrow afternoon at 2:30."

At that meeting, Dr. Martine gave Colleen the address of Dr. Baker, a local orthodontist who offered her a job in his office in return for orthodontics. She started work immediately. The hours were flexible and the work was easy. She still had time for class and a few days' work at the restaurant. Raoul was never mentioned and Colleen didn't ask.

Dr. Baker took x-rays and within weeks Colleen's smile looked and felt like a barbed-wire fence. If Dr. Baker used one rubber band on her braces, she added a second; on the day of her appointment, she always switched back to one.

Every time he complimented her on her remarkable progress she said, "When can they come off?" There was no one her age in the waiting room. There was no one with braces in her classes, or in the bars. Through the summer, one hot boring day after another, Colleen stayed in school.

Then everything changed. In October of 1962 the Cuban Missile Crisis made school irrelevant. Day and night the rumble of military convoys rattled windows and filled the air with dust. Miles of khaki trucks carried somber young men wearing camo, whose dull eyes appraised the tanned coeds they were supposed to protect from Russian missiles. Cuba was just ninety miles from the Florida coastline, and the possibility of nuclear war caused a huge spike in drug and alcohol use.

Everyday Colleen heard about someone who had quit school to join the Army, or left campus to spend the end of days with his parents, or couples who had gone camping—a euphemism for wild behavior, since they had no future. Colleen took up smoking in a world-weary affected way, as did many others. Bars were packed, and the library was empty.

Colleen went to see Dr. Baker. "I'd like to have my braces removed."

"Why?"

"If a bomb drops, I don't want them on. I can't become a spy if I'm unable to disguise myself."

The doctor ruminated. "I'll tell you where I live. If the bomb drops, you can come to my house and I will take them off. Right now is not a good time."

"What if l can't get to your house, or if the house is nothing but a hole in the ground? I'm sorry, but I want them off now."

Dr. Baker folded his arms and thought. "I'll show you how to take them off yourself. You can do it. I'll give you this little gadget to keep with you." He held up a small pair of pliers. "We'll continue as we are, but if you need to do it, you'll be prepared." Then he showed her how to loosen and remove the wires, and after that she kept the little pliers in her purse.

That night after many beers, she called Wilson from the dorm phone. "How are you?"

"Good."

She could hear Edith Piaf singing "*La Vie en Rose*" in the background. "Are you having a party?"

"No. An old friend is here."

Just then Colleen heard a female voice, "Hey, Wild One, come over here."

"That's a misnomer," he said with his hand over the receiver.

Colleen hung up and went back to her room to write a letter to Aunt Charity exaggerating the nuclear survival preparations around her. She described hallways stacked with mason jars of water, boxes of canned tuna, cases of flashlights and lanterns, and her sudden interest in spelunking.

Actually, the worst thing that could happen—a nuclear attack— would take Colleen back to Sheila, a possibility that appealed to her...

in fact it had its advantages. She was getting behind in school, and if the bomb didn't drop soon, she had better start attending her French class. With a schedule that left little time for study, she was lucky she remembered what she heard. Attending class was crucial.

When she went home for Christmas, her parents were astounded by the braces. Edward asked, "Why on earth would you do something so stupid? I thought you were smart. And when are you going to learn something useful? Marie, why don't you teach her how to cook? Teach her something that matters, so she can find a husband."

Colleen answered, "What is there to learn? Anyone who can read a recipe can cook. I don't need to cook any more than I need a husband. I don't see the advantage of either."

In the skirmishes at home, Marie complained continually, but not to Edward. She sighed deeply, because she had difficulty swallowing, and she said her other digestive problems were the result of worry over Edward's drinking.

Colleen and her old friends from high school went to bars in Newport that were full of OC's, Naval Officer Candidates who were college graduates from all parts of the country, who were only there for four months of school. They were primarily interested in a party... drinking, dancing, and meeting girls. She and her friends didn't have more than a beer or two over a long evening of talking and dancing.

They enjoyed the music, and the conversations, because they were entertaining, not fraught with anxiety the way a real boyfriend or a real date would be.

One morning while she drank black coffee, Marie said, "Your father told me that you drink when you go out, but I didn't believe him. Is it true?"

"Yes."

"You promised me you would never drink. I didn't want you to turn out like him."

"I didn't turn out like him."

"Why can't you be more—"

"Like Sheila was?"

"Yes."

"Because, I'm me."

"Promise me you won't drink again."

"No."

"I want you to stay in tonight."

"I'm babysitting for one of my old customers."

"Oh."

Mr. Coddington picked Colleen up to babysit, and at the end of the evening, Colleen asked, "Would you mind dropping me at The Tavern? Some of my friends are there and they will give me a ride home."

10 KEITH

Sitting at the bar, Keith touched his pocket to make sure he really had the letter. It was short. Charlotte was sorry she had ever met him, did not want him to contact her again, and expected him to leave the premises immediately if he accidentally happened upon her anywhere, forever.

The vitriolic letter had been prompted by a simple "Thinking of you" card he had sent to her home, so that she would know he was alright. He had put the card in the mail several days before graduation from flight school, when he thought they had a future together... if she extricated herself from her present situation.

Something about Charlotte was very special, something he had never expected to find. Unfortunately, his hopes that they would end up together were dashed on graduation night when he was attacked by Austin, her husband, and his wingman Rev Snake. Her reaction was predictable and correct. After all, she was a married woman with a child. Still, his fingers lingered on the pocket which held the envelope that her fingers had touched, and he wanted to smell the paper. Reluctantly, he put his hand on the bar.

His feelings for Charlotte had turned him upside down. Unfortunately, he had been unable to resist the passion that urged him to sweep her up and away. In his dreams she was barefoot and waiting for him.

In the light of day, he briefly considered the possibility that she had no idea that they belonged together, but he discarded that notion for one where she suffered and cried over the loss of their love, as he did. Remembering the visit from Austin and Rev Snake, he knew that his romance with Charlotte was over, kaput.

He wondered whether to order a Manhattan or a Michelob. The mess he had left in Pensacola called for a Manhattan, but his budget demanded a draft.

When the door opened, Colleen entered in a swirl of snowflakes and cold wind. All the tables were taken, and she didn't see a familiar face. Stepping up to the bar, she took the empty stool beside Keith, and sat sideways to keep an eye on the door. If someone she knew showed up, she needed to arrange a ride home.

Tim, the bartender, brought her a beer and asked Keith if he needed another. He did. It was his first day off the ship since he'd reported to the USS Forrestal and he had been drinking for a while.

A funny thing happened then. The beer made him chatty and he started talking to Colleen about his mother, a topic he usually avoided. He said he was convinced that men transfer feelings of attachment from their mothers to the women they love. Colleen was a listener by inclination, and her nursing experience enhanced that proclivity. Her quiet attention encouraged him.

He told her about going down the stairs in his old house, how he walked in front of his mother while holding the railing with one hand and dragging a pillow case of matchbox cars with his other hand. His mother tripped on the pillowcase and didn't stop tumbling until she landed at the bottom. When Keith reached her, she looked asleep. In a moment she opened her eyes and asked him to call his father at the office and tell the operator to send help. He stood on a chair and dialed "0" as he had been taught. After telling the operator about his mother, he gave her his father's number at work.

No one was allowed to bother his father, but he came right to the phone.

"Go to your mother," he told Keith. "Tell her I'm on my way, and so is the emergency wagon."

He went back to the stairway with his pillow case and sat down near his mother. There was a little blood in her ear; that was all. She didn't speak. Soon a fireman was there. Then his father took him next door where he stood at the window and watched until the ambulance left with his parents. His mother was on a stretcher.

When Billy, the neighbor's son, came home from school, he told Keith that his mother was having a baby. Keith didn't believe it. He hadn't heard anything about a baby. But the neighbor was right. Later, Billy told him that his mother wasn't coming home because she was dead. He was right about that too.

A few days later, his father brought his sister home and told Keith that his mother had gone to heaven. No one talked about it. They lived in a house with a baby and no mother, and no one remarked on the unnaturalness of it. It was as though she had never been.

Colleen didn't remark on it either. She reached over and put her hand on Keith's.

Without a word, he took her to the tiny dance floor where the crowd parted slightly to absorb them, and a song about people who need people seemed perfect. They occupied a space just large enough to stand and sway. Keith was tall and athletic, a good dancer. After several slow numbers they returned to the bar.

Colleen said, "I need to get going soon. I have to find a ride." She looked around for a familiar face.

"I can walk you home," he said.

"Then what?" she asked.

"Then I'll keep going 'til I get to the base."

"Are you serious? You'll die of hypothermia."

"Probably not, I'm already pickled."

"My house is on the way to the base," she said. "Are you sure you wouldn't rather take a cab?"

"I can't. I spent all my money at the bar," he answered.

Colleen put on her coat and took her babysitting money out of her pocket. "I have some money," she said. "Let's find out what it costs to go to the base with a stop at my house. If we have enough, we will do that. Otherwise, we'll walk."

But just then Colleen saw Carolyn, a fellow townie, and she arranged a ride for both of them.

A bunch of locals, some of whom were boarding students at Salve Regina College, took every seat in the station wagon. Keith and Colleen climbed in the "way back" and pulled their knees close to their chests to conserve body warmth.

Carolyn looked at them in the rearview mirror. "The heat doesn't get back there, so there's a blanket to help. You'll probably need it. You're going to be the last ones I drop off," she said before turning the radio on.

They moved together, spreading the blanket over their coats and up to their faces. It was so cold they leaned forward and breathed inside it. Colleen spoke close to Keith's ear, "How old was your mother when she died?"

"Twenty-nine," he answered.

In the dark under the blanket her voice was a whisper. "I'm sorry."

"It's okay. It was a long time ago. I have no idea what got me talking about it anyway."

Cold and tired, they were quiet for the rest of the ride.

"Here we are," Carolyn said.

Keith climbed over the seat and went outside to open the door to the "way back" for Colleen. Then he walked her to the porch. She reached out to shake his hand but he held hers with both of his and said, "I'll be in touch."

Colleen went back to Florida without seeing him again, but she had given him her address at school, and before long, he sent a card. After that he called often and even came to Gainesville to take her to a Gator football game.

Keith's roommate, Paul, had taken leave for the holidays, and although Keith had the watch, he also had some welcome time alone in their tiny stateroom. The holidays gave him time to think.

Memories of his mother's death brought recollections of Granny Hancock, his father's mother, who came to live with them.

Granny was tough. She had been born with one normal arm and one small, undeveloped one that didn't have a hand. She called it her baby arm. Keith didn't notice it most of the time because her dresses had long sleeves that flared where a cuff would have been. When her arm was at her side it looked natural, because the sleeve ended in the folds of her apron, or was tucked into a pocket. But if she wanted to use the baby arm, she lifted it up, and the sleeve fell back to expose the stump.

What Keith did notice was that her good arm was as strong as steel, a super arm. When he was running around in the house, or making too much noise, or creating a mess, he learned to avoid her. As quick as a flash, she would tuck his sister Tisha under her baby arm and grab him on the fly. Her grip was like an iron trap for wild boys.

Granny used her feet like hands, and she was barefoot in the house most of the time. She could grab him with her hand, push him down on the rug, and hold him there with one foot; he was powerless against her. He couldn't imagine how much it would hurt if she were to hit him with her good arm, and he didn't want to find out.

She demanded good behavior and he was good. To change Tisha, she put a blanket on the rug and held her still with a foot on her chest while using her hand and the other foot to manipulate the diaper and pins. Granny made it look easy. She liked to do more than one thing at a time. She read her favorite movie magazine while she ironed, by turning the pages with her toes. One day Keith stood beside the ironing board and attempted to turn the pages of a book with his toes. It was impossible.

He adored Granny Hancock, feared her, and was fascinated by her. He loved her and loved being her helper. After her bath one night, Keith saw her sitting in her room. The air smelled faintly like the bottles of Evening in Paris on her bureau. She was sitting on her bed in her fluffy robe, powdering her incredibly long and supple feet.

Smooth and cool as polished marble, with delicate blue veins, her feet tickled, subdued, comforted, and restrained Tisha, his baby sister. She played with Granny's toes when she was being changed, and it made Granny giggle.

Keith said, "I want to do that."

Granny refused, "No, you're too old."

"No, I'm not," he insisted.

"You're a big boy," she said.

"No, I'm not," he answered as he lay on the rug beside Tisha, and pulled Granny's foot onto his chest. "I'm just a baby," he said.

Granny briefly tickled him with her foot, and said, "That's all."

She didn't overreact to Keith because she knew it was natural for an older child to have temporary periods of regression when a new baby joins the family. An older sibling might want a binky, or to be fed baby food, or to be rocked to sleep.

Granny was the perfect person to take care of her grandchildren, but within six months of her arrival, she died one morning in church. Keith had not been prepared for his sister's arrival, or his mother's death; now he was devastated by the loss of his grandmother. He was beginning to think it was dangerous to love someone.

Before long, Keith's father married Jane, a wonderful woman who loved boys. But her sons, Charlie and Peter, didn't want another brother and were dead set against sharing their mom. They were quick to tell Keith their mother only pretended to like him. When they moved into Keith's home, they treated him as though he were an unwelcome stranger in their house, not the other way around.

Tisha escaped their torture by running to Jane at the slightest provocation. Keith, used to taking care of himself, was too proud to complain; he endured. When Charlie and Peter realized that he didn't tattle on them, they increased their torment. Their mischief was opportunistic.

If Keith was doing homework at the kitchen table, they spilled milk on it with a smirk. If he left a book unattended, they hid it. He was always hunting for his stuff. If he asked them where they had put his book, they would say, "I don't remember." If someone called him, he was not given the message. If he was in a nearby room when one of them answered the phone, they would say, "He's not here." They hung up rather than call out to him in the next room. If he asked them where Jane was, they answered, "She doesn't want you to bother her."

No matter, Jane loved Keith. He was a godsend with Tisha, his little sister who chattered "Keef" this and "Keef" that all day long. He put her in the wagon with her dolls and books, and gave them rides. When she talked about her doll family, he actually listened. He taught her colors and numbers and nursery rhymes. Keith was an exceptional big brother.

Granny had taught him to help with chores before being asked, and Keith automatically picked up the newspaper, put everyone's shoes away, and took out the trash. He did more than anyone expected, and was less trouble than the other children. Jane appreciated his help, and self-reliance; her boys were demanding and spoiled in comparison. It got worse after she said they should be more like their "big brother."

Keith didn't bring anyone home because he didn't want his friends to be victims of their mischief, or to see how his new "brothers" treated him.

After Granny died, Keith was finished with mother substitutes. Jane was never more than his father's wife to him. He was still cordial, and carried her packages, and put his things away, and tried not to judge. But the human heart is mysterious. You just don't know what you would do, until you walk in someone else's shoes.

Keith learned that it was easier for him to be a girl's friend than for the girl to be his friend. Girls tended to mistake friendship for something more. They presumed he would become more than a friend over time, but he was only interested in the beginning, no matter who the girl was.

Eventually he realized that his interest ended after he saw a girl's feet. To put it bluntly, no matter how beautiful a girl was, she probably had dog feet. Extraordinary, beautiful feet like Granny's were as difficult to encounter as a Sasquatch.

After college he decided to become a naval aviator. The Vietnam War was in full swing and flying from port to port sounded adventurous, in addition to being a sure chance to meet gorgeous girls. The first was his section leader's wife, a former Miss Texas who wore sexy shoes, and was smart, sassy, straight shooting, and funny—everything he wanted in a woman. A pair of red velvet high-heeled open toe pumps with double ankle straps were her favorite. Keith couldn't keep his eyes off them. "Are those shoes comfortable?" he asked.

"Oh yes," she drawled.

"Can I look inside one?"

"Are you serious?" she wondered.

"Yup."

Charlotte's husband, Austin, was late, and she'd had a drink while waiting for him at the section's regular Friday night Happy Hour. Everyone else had been at the big table in the back for an hour. They were now playing a game with vodka shots that promised to get rowdy. Charlotte slipped her shoe off and passed it under the table to Keith. He had begun to study feet... and shoes.

He couldn't help himself. The shoe still radiated her body warmth. His fingers slipped inside, then through the peek-a-boo toe box, he felt the vamp, the instep, the smooth inner sole, the underside of the straps. A glance at her foot under the table told him he would be happy with those toes forever. Then he turned the shoe over; the sole indicated it was formed on a curved last, a thin connection between the heel and the ball of the foot that gave the shoe flexibility and comfort. A curved last meant a high arch. He sighed.

"What are you doing with my wife's shoe?" Austin asked as he took the seat Charlotte had saved for him.

From the other end of the table, his wingman, Reverend Snake answered, "He has been pestering her to try it on!"

"Woooohoooo!" The shouts and laughter drowned out everyone's conversation. "Here it is, just what you want," Keith tossed the shoe to Wildcat.

"Woooohoooo!" The volume increased.

Wildcat brought the shoe to Charlotte and knelt at her chair to put it on. "Okay, okay. Let's see if it fits, Cinderella."

"Get away from her." Austin pushed Wildcat out of the way, and knelt down to put the shoe on.

Keith ordered a round for the table. The fact that Charlotte was married to his classmate hadn't entered his mind. She was the mother of a beautiful little girl who reminded him of Tisha when she was a toddler, and he had fallen for both of them from a great height. He crashed with a smile, and although his thoughts made no sense, he was a happy man.

As though Austin didn't exist, Keith wanted Charlotte and the baby to be his. He wanted to cook pancakes for them the way Granny taught him. He imagined himself in a toy department at Christmas. When he ran into Charlotte on base, he offered to push her carriage, or carry her packages to the car.

One day when he saw her in line at the gas station, he stopped to pump her gas. She had just had her nails done and was grateful. Later, he ran into her at a men's store and helped her pick out a Father's Day gift for Austin. She must have mentioned it, because Austin was clearly annoyed when he grabbed Keith the next day, and told him to stay away from his family.

Keith was shocked. He had accidentally run into Charlotte, and happened to help her pick out Austin's Father's Day gift. What was the problem? The fact that he might have a crush on her wasn't a problem at all; it was just a harmless fantasy. But the air was thinner when she was in his vicinity, and he was on edge. He could only do one thing at a time, breathe or swallow.

Charlotte noticed his reactions, and it threw her for a loop. She couldn't imagine how she could possibly be happily married to Austin, yet be aware of someone else. She concluded that her marriage had to be lacking in a fundamental way.

The more they tried to avoid each other, the less possible it seemed. When she decided to leave her husband, she called Keith and asked him to meet her for coffee. She brought the baby with her. Hopelessly in love, Keith had never been alone with her, had not even kissed her.

He rectified that omission in the coffee shop, ending the kiss when the proprietor brought the menus to the booth and said, "Get a room."

They did. They turned on cartoons for the baby, and as they turned to hug each other, they fell on top of the bed. The "Bang" of a door slamming nearby brought Charlotte back to reality. She jerked her head to look at the door as though Austin was going to walk in. "What was that?" she said.

"I didn't hear anything," Keith said, with her foot in both hands.

"I need to go!" she said with alarm.

"Not yet." Keith kissed her instep. Her feet were glorious. Her second toe was just slightly shorter than the big one and the nails were painted lavender. He had been waiting since he was a little boy to see toes like these, and he was going to kiss one if it killed him.

"Weirdo! Let go of me." She pulled her foot away.

"Please, Charlotte." He lunged to reclaim her soft baby-smooth heel.

"No! No!"

Keith had never been in a situation more embarrassing or awkward.

The baby was no longer interested in *Sesame Street,* and wanted to be picked up. "Keef, Keef," she said, turning to him with plump arms extended. Keith experienced the chill of nervous sweat. Buttoning his uniform, he gathered toys with one hand and held the baby with the other while Charlotte ran into the bathroom and composed herself. She took the baby to her car and Keith followed with the child's gear. He stood in the cloud of dust and apologized as she left.

He was definitely sorry; he had totally misjudged her. Emotion ruined everything. It was a mistake to be so involved, to come on too strong and scare her. The following day he heard that Charlotte had flown back to Texas to see a marriage counselor.

Keith was relieved that it was the last week of flight school and he would move to his new duty station immediately. While he hoped that Charlotte had not mentioned any of this to Austin, he remained poised for an explosion. When the big blast didn't happen, he counted the hours until graduation, and safety. He wanted nothing more than to get away from this mess in one piece.

On his last night in Pensacola, after the ceremony and a farewell party where he became thoroughly inebriated, he went back to the barracks and lay down on his bunk. Finally, he could relax.

A few hours later someone stuffed a gag in his mouth. Nearby, a muffled voice said, "Don't make a sound, pervert." Two men wearing black ski masks pulled him out of his bunk and tied a blindfold over his eyes.

After dragging him to the utility room, they pushed him onto a wooden chair, and tied it to a metal support. They pulled his arms behind him, and secured his wrists around the column. A heavy cardboard box was shoved against the chair and they put his feet inside it. Dripping with sweat, he struggled to scream, but the voice near his ear hissed, "Go ahead, stupid."

He recognized the twang.

Austin said, "How about a little music, Rev?"

And the sound of a radio echoed through the barracks.

No doubt about it, Charlotte had told her husband.

Austin's wingman, Reverend Snake, had been raised on a remote mountain in West Virginia where a traveling preacher handled snakes. Rev was his assistant. Rev's parents were hippies who smoked so many mushrooms they thought it was cool for their son to commune with nature through invertebrates.

The rustling sound was very close. A rough burlap bag brushed against him before it was dropped in the box. Through the scratchy fabric Keith could feel the solid strength of the snake's body as it coiled, whipped around, and slithered back to a tight spiral before whipping around again. He tried to pull his bare feet out of the box, but the top was double-taped around his knees.

"How many snakes do you have, Rev?" Austin asked.

"Only two, but they're big."

There was a new sound. Rattling.

Keith began to shiver. He didn't remember ever being so cold. His whole body shook and jerked involuntarily.

"Look, he's having a fit," the Rev said.

"So what?"

"I don't want to be charged with murder," the Rev answered.

"I don't mind," Austin said. He tipped the box to make the snake slither over Keith's bare feet.

Keith jumped straight up, still tied to the chair, which landed on its side... the snakes and Keith's feet were still in the box.

The Rev and Austin began to laugh.

They released Keith's hands so he could take the gag and blindfold off. Austin and the Rev held up two baby rattles, and shook them.

Keith's ragged breathing sounded like a Clydesdale after running the Kentucky Derby.

"Don't take things so serious. Rat snakes are not poisonous," the Rev chuckled.

He picked up a huge black snake and put it back in the bag. Then he put the bag in the box with the rattles.

The Rev and Austin turned to leave with the box.

"This never happened, did it?" Austin said, over his shoulder.

"Nnnoo," Keith choked.

Keith graduated at the top of his class. The insane death-defying thrill he experienced as his airplane was catapulted off a bouncing runway in the middle of the ocean and returned to land on that same impossibly short landing strip, if a steel arresting wire catches the plane's tailhook, would continue as long as he was in the Navy. And if pictures of sexy shoes, and the beautiful feet they romanticized, calmed his nerves when they wound tighter than a tourniquet... *so what*? He was okay with it.

11 ADELINE AND AMBERJEAN

After graduation, Adeline and her whole family was crammed into her room as she packed and tried to prepare Amberjean for her first ear appointment. They were in a rush, and it wasn't going well. It got worse when Amberjean had a tantrum because her mother tried to brush her hair; the child was very protective of her ears.

Regina, Adeline's best friend at school, was a baby expert who knew at a glance what to do. She put Amberjean's stuffed lamb on the bed, and said, "SHHHH." In the hush that followed, she examined the lamb's ears with her fingers, her magnifying glass, and finally, her stethoscope. She knelt on the floor, took off her cap, and pulled her hair back. Putting Amberjean's small fingers around the magnifying glass, she held it near her own ear. Amberjean examined first Regina's and Adeline's ears, then Mamma Dot's and finally PaMa's big hairy ones. By then, she was giggling.

When Regina indicated that it was Amberjean's turn, the child pushed her hair away from her ear-buds and laid her head on the bed. An hour later she quietly submitted to Dr. Romano's examination. He showed them an album of "before" and "after" pictures, a gallery of smiling children who had been transformed by his surgery. He assured Adeline there were new techniques being studied that would improve results even more. Amberjean couldn't take her eyes off the pictures of formerly earless children like her, that now had ears.

Helen Keller said that blindness separates you from things, but deafness separates you from people. Language and speech are developed by hearing. Babies normally learn fifteen hundred words between birth and four years of age. Without ears, Amberjean would not learn the words to share her thoughts and feelings.

There were very few playmates near her grandparents' farm, and most members of her small family circle communicated with each other, ignoring her. As a consequence, her vocabulary was severely limited and delayed. She was an introspective, serious little girl. All that changed when Adeline accepted a job in the delivery room of Newport Hospital. They moved into a converted attic apartment nearby, and Amberjean bloomed. Adeline's hands loved to touch her baby, to smooth her hair and pull her close.

Mrs. Benson, who babysat, was only three doors away. Her stairwell was lined with years of school pictures of children whose parents were all hospital workers. Besides Amberjean, she took care of Katie, who was six months old, and Theresa, a sunny eight year old whose deaf cousin had taught her how to sign.

Exuding cheerful encouragement, Mrs. Benson gave Amberjean confidence, just as Katie's antics and Theresa's lively company banished her loneliness. A light had been turned on inside her and she glowed.

Adeline had seen deaf babies in the hospital respond with joy when their mothers touched them forehead to forehead and hummed. The last thing she did every night was bend her head to touch Amberjean's forehead with her own as she hummed and prayed for her daughter's future.

When PaMa and Mama Dot came to visit, they enjoyed being "walk-ons" on the Jamestown Ferry, or having ice cream at the Newport Creamery, and taking a ride around the Ocean Drive... where they stopped at Brenton's Reef to watch the waves and sea birds.

Amberjean was happy. She had a toy guitar she pretended to play when her mother listened to music on the radio. She learned to sign, and print her name. There was no question that she understood her books and was learning to read.

Wherever Adeline went, whether alone, with Amberjean, or with her parents, the population of Newport was oversupplied with young men in uniform. Officer Candidates, or Jag students (young lawyers in Justice School), or young enlisted men going through training for the Navy, or the Seabees, were at the Creamery, in the park, on the beach, and in the stores. Occasionally homesickness prompted them to initiate a conversation with local civilians.

One day the Fraziers were approached by a handsome young man in uniform who was a "walk-on," riding the Jamestown Ferry back and forth, just like they were. David Shaw was no longer the skinny towhead they remembered from their neighborhood.

When he recognized Adeline and her parents, he greeted them like long-lost relatives. They would not have recognized him, since he now towered above them and (Adeline thought) filled out his uniform like a recruitment poster.

He explained that he joined the Navy and had been trained as a construction mechanic in the Seabees. Now he was in Newport for further training. After chatting briefly with Mr. and Mrs. Frazier about his family, he asked Adeline if she wanted to climb the ladder to the wheelhouse deck. She did, and before the ferry stopped, he had her phone number.

Although she didn't expect to hear from him, he called the next day to invite her and the baby out for ice cream. As they walked, David asked if she was still involved with Amberjean's father.

"I never was," she answered.

He waited as she told him about the Anderson Mill clambake. Rather than say too much about her drunkenness, she focused her explanation on the deaf boy that people had been picking on all day. "Like Amberjean, he didn't have ears. He was drunk, sitting on a blanket, and crying. I tripped over his feet, and I fell on him, he grabbed me and rolled over on top of me. We were both crying. I patted his head, to get his attention so that he would let me up. I was dizzy and sick and couldn't stop him. As quick as I could, I got away and took the boat back to the city."

David said, "Did you tell anyone?"

"No."

"What did you say to your parents?"

"I told them that I'd had too much to drink and I didn't know what was happening. I told the truth, that I'd never done anything like that before."

"What did they say?"

"That I was a tramp without the sense of a turnip, and they wanted to force someone to marry me."

"How did you handle that?"

"I said I didn't love anyone, and I wouldn't get married."

"Was that the end of it?"

"No. I told my boss that my mother was very sick, and I was needed on the farm. Then my boss told a guy who had asked me out a few times and was at the clambake. His name was Frisco. He came to the farm to see me, but I had already moved to Aunt Janet's in Swansea. My parents thought he was my boyfriend, and they told him where I was. Then he came to my aunt's house, in fact, he came often, and tried to talk me into marrying him."

"Did you?"

"No, of course not."

"Where is he now?"

"He came to the hospital to see me when I had the baby, but I was still under anesthesia. He went to the nursery window and when he saw Amberjean's ears, he left. I haven't heard from him since that day."

They started walking again... in silence.

Then David said, "Adeline, you were raped on that beach."

She had said she *couldn't* stop him. She'd meant to say she *didn't* stop him. Small difference. Large difference.

Becoming drunk was the worst mistake of her life; it ended in sex with the earless boy. And now an earless little girl held her hand and David's hand and jumped between them. This was the time to clear up all misunderstandings, confess all.

But she didn't want to talk about it anymore. Maybe if she had tried to stop the encounter, it would have turned out the same. Maybe she hadn't known what to do. Maybe David had heard as much truth as he could absorb, and had now chosen what he wanted to believe.

And what difference did it make, anyway? Adeline left their conversation and its lost details in the past. Her eyes were filled with emotion.

David looked at her. "What is it?"

She couldn't say it, but the worst mistake of her life—drunken sex with an earless dunce—was also the best thing that ever happened to her. Amberjean gave her life a purpose, made the ordinary special and wonderful. The baby added love and beauty to her days. Her moral failure had created a beautiful little girl she would die for... but she couldn't say that while looking into the eyes of the only man she would ever love.

"Thank you," she said.

"For what?"

"For not telling me I'm as stupid as a turnip."

They were talking over Amberjean's head while holding the child's hands and swinging her. "Let's go up the hill," he said and swooped the child onto his shoulders.

When he looked at Adeline, his eyes said everything she needed to know.

Within a year, David and Adeline were married in a simple ceremony at the Naval Chapel in Newport, attended only by their parents, grandparents, and Amberjean. A few days later, David left to join a Seabee battalion in the Far East.

Adeline and Amberjean planned to meet him in Port Hueneme, California, when he returned. In the meantime, they stayed in Newport, where Amberjean spent her whole life in pursuit of communicating. First, she learned signing, then reading, and finally, speaking... but that wasn't enough. Her doctors, nurses, speech therapists, mother, grandparents, teachers, and friends, all wanted her to be able to hear. They were more anxious for it than she was.

She knew that if she said she would be happier leaving things as they were, they would be disappointed. Thoughts like that made her feel guilty. She loved her mother so much, she sometimes had nightmares about losing her. She was afraid that her mother wouldn't be happy with just one little girl, even after that one could hear. She would want children with ears already attached, children fathered by David.

Secretly, she prayed her real father would find her.

Before Adeline married David, she told Amberjean her father was killed in the war, but she gave no details. In fact, her mother was so upset when she talked about him, that Amberjean didn't mention it for a long time.

When some of the children at school talked about going to visit family graves on Memorial Day, Amberjean wanted to go to her own daddy's grave. Adeline said they couldn't because he was missing; there was no grave.

Amberjean started to pray that he would be found, and he would come to find her. She prayed that David would find her daddy, if his plane had crashed and floated that far.

She thought her father may have been captured, or lost his memory. Secretly, she worried about him a lot. And she wanted a picture of him. But her mother didn't have any pictures. She said although he was handsome, he didn't like to have his picture taken. He wanted to wait to have a big wedding after the war. Adeline had agreed.

Amberjean didn't have his last name because he didn't know Adeline was pregnant, and they hadn't expected to make a baby. And Adeline wouldn't tell anyone his name because he didn't know he was a father, and she had wanted to wait and be the first to tell him.

It took Amberjean a long time to realize that she not only didn't know her father's last name or his first name, but she also didn't know where he was born, or anything else. When she went to Boston for ear reconstruction, she brought her guitar. It helped occupy her when she felt alone and damaged, and missed having a father.

In the hospital, Amberjean saw other fathers shake the doctor's hand and say, "Take good care of my little girl." She believed that the doctors were especially careful not to hurt the little girls who had fathers, and she wanted a daddy to talk to her doctor for her. In fact when she told Dr. J. her problem, he took a special interest in her.

He said, "You are a lucky girl, because I'm going to bring my guitar to work so I can play with you, and I know more than anybody's daddy about ears, and I am here to take care of you just like your real daddy wants me too."

Amberjean clapped her hands, and Adeline blew her nose.

The scar where her rib cartilage was removed, healed quickly. Then the shape of her ears was visible under the stretched skin on the sides of her head, like something in a frosted-glass display case. After Amberjean's skin settled into its curves, the next surgery projected her ears from her head. By the time her hair grew back, her hearing was ninety percent of normal, her speech deficits had been greatly improved by therapy, and most important of all, with her hair down she looked like everyone else at school. She was also getting very good at playing the guitar.

Adeline had a few close friends who waited with her during Amberjean's surgeries and worried with her during the difficult days of David's extended deployment. By necessity, communication was limited, and the Seabee wives shared bits of information they had with each other. It was a very relieved and excited group when they were sure that the ship had turned toward home.

When David returned this time, they would try to have another child. He wanted a larger family, and Adeline wanted that too. A little brother or sister would be good for Amberjean.

When Adeline noticed that her breast was swollen, she tried not to panic. She knew lumps were usually harmless cysts, or calcium deposits. Benign, usually. But this wasn't a lump; it was a generalized swelling, and a slight rash.

The doctor insisted on an immediate biopsy. By the time David received a letter about it, the biopsy would be over. What could he do anyway? He was on his way home; he could only worry, and she was doing that already.

Adeline decided to think positively and did not tell him. That meant she couldn't tell the other wives, because if one of them slipped up and mentioned it in a letter, David would find out third hand... a horrible way to get bad news.

Adeline had heard about information passed along innocently, wreaking marital havoc. Luckily, no wives lived nearby; distance made secrets easier to keep. Amberjean was another case. Explaining the need for a hospital procedure would be tough. The whole truth included the possibility that Adeline might leave the hospital mutilated and disfigured, in a fight for her life. There was no way to think about that, and no way to prepare Amberjean, or anyone else, for the unthinkable.

It was standard practice to rush patients to biopsy, and from biopsy to mastectomy, before they returned to consciousness. Speed was considered necessary to minimize the cancer's spread. Both her grandmother and aunt had died of breast cancer. Adeline knew the possibility of cancer would send Mama Dot into a tailspin, but she had no choice. The word *biopsy* was never far from her thoughts; it was a difficult and powerful word.

Making plans as though everything was routine, and the results would be negative, she asked Mama Dot to take care of Amberjean while she checked herself into the hospital. When malignant results were confirmed by pathology during the biopsy, the surgeon performed a radical mastectomy immediately.

The Halsted procedure, named for the doctor who developed the technique in the 1880s, was radical. It removed the chest muscles, pectoralis major and minor, and the mammary, supraclavicular, and axillary lymph nodes. Although extreme, it was the gold standard for breast cancer treatment until the 1970s.

For a patient who came into the hospital for the biopsy of a small lump, waking up from anesthesia was either a matter of ecstasy or despair. Excessive dissection, coupled with the diagnosis of cancer, shattered hope and spirits. When Adeline became aware of pain and stiffness, drains and tubes, she closed her eyes to the horror, and tried to return to unconsciousness. Unfortunately, her nightmare was real.

Mama Dot tried to reassure an inconsolable Amberjean, who was overwhelmed by her mother's sudden surgery. Things came to a head when Mama Dot's terror-filled eyes expressed a growing fear that her daughter was dying, and she hyperventilated until she passed out. One of the nurses put her in a wheelchair and brought her to the emergency room. After checking her blood pressure and vital signs, the doctor diagnosed "panic attack" and gave her a mild tranquilizer and a prescription.

Mama Dot was at the hospital every day, leaving only to pick Amberjean up after school, and bring her back. One quiet morning, Adeline asked her mother to take care of Amberjean when she died.

Refusing to entertain such depressing thoughts, Mama Dot said, "You are getting better, and we're not going to talk about something that's not going to happen."

Undeterred, Adeline said, "I don't want it to happen. I know it might not happen. But if it does, will you take care of Amberjean?"

"Of course... I would, if David wanted me to."

"It's not how David feels that is important. When it comes to this, it's how Amberjean feels that matters."

Mama Dot paused and changed the subject. "I think I should get some yarn and teach Amberjean to crochet."

Adeline looked up. "Mama, I have an old diary in my sewing basket. It's locked, but the key is in the desk drawer. If anything happens to me, please take it, and give it to Amberjean when you think she's old enough."

"Oh my God, Adeline! What is wrong with you today? Stop this crazy talk."

"I mean it, Mama. Promise me."

"Okay. I promise, but only if you stop this talk right now." When Mama Dot left the hospital that afternoon, she was more disturbed by her daughter's conversation than by Adeline's diagnosis of metastatic inflammatory breast cancer.

David arrived in time to bring Adeline home from the hospital. She sat in the front seat, blinking at the intense blue of the sky, amazed at the cars all around her. People acted as though it was a normal day, but her diagnosis was a death sentence, and she knew the end of her world was near.

When they drove up to the front door of the farmhouse, she saw the "Welcome Home Mommy" sign colored by Amberjean, and taped into place by Mama Dot.

"We'll do a lot of coloring together, and maybe you can teach me to play guitar," she said before she realized she should not talk of a future she didn't have. She didn't want to leave Amberjean with broken promises and disappointment.

The next morning David brought her a breakfast tray of orange juice, scrambled eggs, and tea. Adeline patted the bed and said, "Go get your coffee and come back to keep me company."

In those few seconds, when she moved to straighten the covers and make room for David on the bed, a blood clot broke loose from the side of the femoral vein in her leg. Drawn into the current of Adeline's bloodstream like a clump of mud on a riverbank being pulled into a creek, the clot raced toward her lung.

Amberjean appeared in the doorway just as Adeline sat up in an effort to catch her breath... and dropped back to the pillow, lifeless.

Mama Dot screamed for help, and David rushed in to start CPR, but when the paramedics arrived, they confirmed what was apparent. She was gone. They eventually learned the cause of death was pulmonary embolism.

David had come home from Korea in time to plan his wife's funeral. Alone in Adeline's childhood bedroom, he sat with his heart full of confusion and foreboding.

Mama Dot put Adeline's diary and its key in her sewing box, without mentioning their existence to anyone.

Adeline was buried beside her grandparents at St. John's Cemetery in Attleboro. It had only been a few weeks since her diagnosis, only a few months since Amberjean's most recent ear surgery, and only a short time since she had been anticipating David's return... a time happier than any she ever had in her whole life.

The lines on Mama Dot's face deepened, and her expression held no memory of a smile. Catching sight of herself in a mirror or store window, she was surprised at how old she had become. Before David left, he signed a document appointing Mama Dot as Amberjean's guardian. Then he was off to Port Hueneme and back to the Seabees.

He had been assigned another tour in the Far East. He returned to work that turned days into nights, and demanded his total attention. He had no idea what else to do. Amberjean was safe and well with her grandparents, and rather than raise the issue of adopting her, he left it for the future.

Back with her grandparents, Amberjean took comfort in the farm. She loved her room with its familiar bed, covered by the quilt she had helped to sew. The pink and white checked wallpaper consoled her. At school, her teacher held her hand and brought her to her desk, and the class welcomed her enthusiastically.

She spent hours with her grandmother, visiting memories of her mother's short life. They played Adeline's radio, and lit her ballerina lamp when the winter sun disappeared early in the afternoon. Amberjean wore her mother's resized imitation birthstone ring and Mama Dot wore Adeline's watch. Amberjean took her pink imitation cashmere scarf, and Mama Dot wore her gloves.

"What do you think we should do with the rest of your mother's things?" Mama Dot asked one day.

"What do you mean?" Amberjean wanted to know.

"I've been thinking that we might want to invite your Aunt Janet, and a few others who loved your mother, to come here and see if there are any of her clothes they would like. Unless you don't agree," Mama Dot said.

"I don't want anyone else to have them."

"Okay. How about having Thanksgiving dinner here and letting them see your mother's photo albums?" To this Amberjean agreed, and helped Mama Dot get ready. They polished the furniture, organized the closet and drawers, the shoes, the accessories, the costume jewelry, the books, and the knick-knacks.

After the men and boys were stuffed with turkey dinner, they took a break by heading to the barn to check on a new calf. The women and girls gathered in Adeline's room, and sat on the bed to listen to her records. Amberjean played her guitar. The youngest girls played dress-up with her hats and necklaces, while Janet looked through photo albums and told a hysterical story about Adeline's short career as a beautician. Everyone had a story to tell, and they had a wonderful day.

12 NOVEMBER 22, 1963

The loudspeaker on the hallway ceiling dropped words as hard as rocks. "President Kennedy has been shot."

Colleen threw her peanut butter and jelly sandwich into the trash and stepped into the third-floor hallway. What she had just heard was inconceivable. Doors opened and girls stood looking at each other and the PA system.

The loudspeaker in Grove Hall crackled again. "I repeat, President Kennedy was shot in Dallas, Texas, this morning. There are no further details at this time."

Colleen wondered if this was the beginning of a war, or a coup d'etat. She hurried outside into the stream of students walking in the direction of her next class. Turning to the girl beside her she asked, "Did you hear that the President was shot?"

"Yes, someone came into my last class and gave a note to the professor, then made an announcement. The professor grabbed his papers and left. Then we left too."

"I wonder how seriously he's wounded. Was there any information after the announcement?"

"Not a word. You could hear a pin drop."

It didn't seem possible that someone would shoot the President.

His youth and vitality should have protected him, his wealth and power should have prevented it. What kind of person would raise a weapon against the President of the United States? How could anyone in the world be safe, if he was not?

Usually the noise of students walking, calling, talking, chewing, and chattering, filled the air along the pathways and in the hallways with an unintelligible din. Today students walked in silence, footsteps muffled. Even the air was shocked still.

But some classes continued, some birds flew, and radio announcers changed the word "shot" to "assassinated." Crops grew, flowers bloomed, babies were born, mothers made dinner, kids played ball, and people stood at bus stops.

Colleen was surprised. She expected something more, a dangerous unknown consequence to befall the nation. Anticipating its occurrence, she stopped at the Draft and Dog, where she ran into a classmate.

"I'm so upset," she started.

"Me too. I was driving on Gainesville Boulevard and when I came to a four-way stop, all the cars stopped around me. They had their windows open and I could hear the announcements on one radio station after another. It was so weird. No one moved. We all got out of our cars and stood there. Some of us were crying. After a few minutes we got back into our cars and drove away. I still can't believe it."

"I was at his wedding," Colleen said.

"What?" asked a voice nearby.

"It was in Newport, Rhode Island. That's my hometown. It was at St. Mary's church. A huge wedding, with famous people from all over the world. My friends and I waited behind a barricade for hours to see Jackie in her wedding dress get out of the limo and go into the church," Colleen elaborated.

"Come with us," someone said. "I'll make us Cuba Libres and we'll remember Kennedy." Someone bought a bologna and brought it with them to make sandwiches. They were a bunch of random students. One guy's father was a pilot who had flown JFK once, when he was a Senator. JFK went into the cockpit to ask for a smooth ride. He said his back didn't like too much bouncing. He flirted with the stewardess, too.

The Cuba Libres were so good, they had another. Colleen said, "He was married on September 12, 1953."

"How do you know?" someone asked.

"I told you. I was there. My friends and I waited for that day like we were getting married ourselves. My mother worked at the reception. More than twelve hundred people ate outside on the lawn overlooking the sea at Hammersmith Farm, the Auchincloss estate. Almost everyone in Newport worked on that wedding."

"What did your mother do?"

"She was a server. So was my aunt, but because her feet hurt, she told someone she was a cook and they believed her. They let her be someone's assistant. Every lobsterman in town was sold out. My mother brought home a piece of the wedding cake wrapped in a napkin that I put under my pillow... but I ate it before breakfast."

Someone said, "Let's have those bologna sandwiches."

"Okay," Colleen said. It was getting dark and she hadn't eaten since breakfast.

Then someone put Peter, Paul, & Mary records in the stack and people began to fall asleep.

In the middle of the night Colleen woke up. Several girls she knew were up and moving around, pacing. "Are you awake?" they asked.

"Yes, what's the matter?"

"We're planning what we're going to do when we graduate."

"Are you kidding?" Colleen asked.

"This is my last semester," someone said. "Everyone has a plan. You should too."

"I'm going to join the Navy and volunteer for a job as an advisor on a swift boat in the Mekong Delta," a familiar voice said.

"Why, Wilson?"

Colleen wondered how long he had been there.

"High adventure and danger. Great experience for a book about the war, if I write one. Good way to prepare for a job as a spy. All or none of the above," he answered.

"Go back to the danger," someone else said.

"That's what I was thinking about. I don't want anyone back here waiting for me. That would change everything—I'd probably hide behind trees, throw a white towel in the air, and surrender every time I heard a gun go off."

"What about me?" Colleen wondered why she had spoken.

"I'll write to you and you'll write to me, and we'll leave the future to fate."

"Fate might not be kind," she answered.

"That's the reason tonight is important," someone else remarked.

"Why?" Colleen wanted to know.

"Because Kennedy died today, and if he could give us advice right now, he would say, 'Don't waste a minute of your life. The future is not guaranteed'."

Colleen didn't recognize the voice.

She turned to leave and people were sleeping all over the place. Wilson had a blanket and pillow on the floor.

He spoke in French, "Think of how you will feel if I die. Come snuggle with me."

They lay together, and wondered about the day, and the future. Then he whispered words that sounded like poetry, or music, and they fell asleep. The darkness and the light blanket covered them. It was warm and safe and quiet and even the ceiling fan was slow.

Just before dawn Colleen woke and grabbed her shoes and purse and snuck out of the house.

Back at her dorm she put on her pajamas and went back to sleep. When the hall phone rang and one of the girls called her name, she ignored it. Later she got up and went to class. When she returned there was a message pinned to her door.

"Call me," it said. She threw it away. She was afraid to see Wilson again. She ignored his phone messages for a few days, and he came to her dorm to see her. She asked one of the girls to go to the reception area to tell him she wasn't there.

Then he showed up at the restaurant where she worked. She told the owner she was sick and ran out the back door, and all the way to her dorm while he sat and waited for her at a table.

She ran into him at the bookstore. She dropped what she had in her hand and hurried out. He followed saying, "Wait, wait up." But she didn't wait. She went faster and faster until she was running and he was out of sight. Soon it was the end of the semester and he was gone.

At her regular appointment with Dr. Baker, he said, "Are you going home for Christmas?"

"Yes, five of us sharing the driving and the cost of gas, we leave next Wednesday."

"Want to get your braces off before you go?"

"Do you mean it? When?"

"If you give me back my little pliers, how about today?"

Colleen almost levitated out of the dental chair. Back at Grove Hall, a broadly smiling Colleen ran into her dorm neighbor, Louise, who worked part time in the Administration Office. As a side benefit, the job familiarized her with valuable information helpful to navigating the educational process. In addition, Colleen noted that Louise was adept at securing financial help for herself, and Colleen was eager to learn more about that. At the moment Louise was applying to become an exchange student.

"Want me to bring you an application?" she asked.

The next day Colleen filled out an application for a "Summer with Shakespeare" program at Cambridge that included financial assistance. Her cost, including transportation, would be no different than University of Florida and she would earn nine credit hours.

Going to Cambridge was more exciting than anything she had ever imagined for herself. When she called Marie and Edward to discuss it, she told them that it was the kind of thing that Sheila would have done if she had lived. But her parents thought it didn't sound legit, and they didn't believe it would really happen. They insisted no good would come of it.

Colleen was disappointed, but heeded their dire admonitions after her father told her, "Stay with your own kind. Don't risk being alone and stuck in a foreign country."

"Besides," he continued. "You make your mother too nervous with your cockamamie ideas."

At Christmastime, when they changed drivers, Colleen was the one who drove through New York like a bat out of hell, they said. She didn't say that her mother was in the hospital again, and she was afraid Marie would die before she arrived. As it turned out, her timing was perfect. When she touched Marie's hand, her mother's eyes opened and her face radiated a love that glowed in the dim hospital light. At that moment she began to improve.

Two days later, Colleen stopped at Frasch's Bakery on her way into the hospital and bought a mocha cake for the nurses.

"Colleen!"

Wilson stood in front of the bakery doorway, blocking it. She didn't need to ask what he was doing in Newport. He was wearing a Navy uniform.

"How long will you be in town?" he asked.

"A few more days. Right now my mother is sick, and I'm on my way across the street to the hospital."

When a customer opened the door to come in, Wilson stepped aside. Colleen slipped by him and he followed her outside.

"What's your number? Can't you take a break, long enough to have a drink, or a sandwich?"

"I don't think so." She walked faster and so did he.

"Colleen, why did you run away?" They were at the front steps of the hospital.

"I have to go. It was good to see you. Congratulations on graduation." Her voice and her smile were sincere.

"I'll call," he said.

Colleen went to the nurses' station and left the cake along with a thank you note signed with her mother's name. Realizing that she had been squeezing the box to smithereens, she hoped when it was opened, the contents still resembled a cake. Frasch's mocha was Marie's favorite and every time a nurse thanked her, it would give her mother a lift. She loved to feed people.

But the thought of having to explain her behavior made her want to stretch out her arms and fly around the room. Sitting in a chair and having a conversation wasn't possible. No matter how she tried to remain calm, she felt the way a wild horse does when the corral gate slams and someone with a bridle approaches. By the time she got home, there was a message for her, with a phone number. She discarded it.

That night when Colleen went to visit Marie, her cousin Christine was there with Marie's older sister, Aunt Lorraine. The sisters did not get along, and avoided each other except in a crisis.

"Why didn't you let me know you were sick?" Lorraine wondered.

"What could you do about it?" Marie replied.

"Maybe I could have helped."

"How? What are you? A doctor now?"

"Why do you have that attitude? You are just like you were as a kid, a smart aleck," Lorraine said.

"I was not. I was mad that you blamed me when you threw away our mother's birthstone ring."

"You took it, and it was never seen again," Lorraine insisted.

"You saw me hide it in the sock drawer and you went behind me and threw the sock away. You know you did," Marie declared.

"You are a crazy woman. Why would I do that? I saw you fooling around with the socks and I cleaned out the drawer, but I never threw any jewelry away. I got rid of a few single socks," Lorraine said. "That's all!"

"Our mother never got over it, Lorraine. She held it against me our whole lives. You threw away her ring, and she blamed *me*."

Christine rolled her eyes at Colleen. "Goodnight, Aunt Marie," she said, as soon as one of them took a breath. "And get well soon... and goodnight, Mom. Colleen will take me home."

Walking to the car Christine said, "I hate it when they fight like that."

Colleen replied, "It's the way they normally fight. Maybe it means my mother is feeling better."

"Let's hope. Want to stop at The Tavern and see who's in town?" Christine asked.

Before the Tavern door closed, Marisa and Ginny waved them over. They hadn't seen each other in almost a year. Marisa's fine platinum hair had grown long and when she dipped her head, it swung over her Slavic features, shielding her from view. A shy and skinny brain in high school, she held herself as though she were trying to disappear.

Since the wild popularity of Peter, Paul, & Mary, she had been mistaken for Mary several times. Recently, someone driving by in a car caught a glimpse of her with her head down and hair shimmering, and shouted, "There's Mary!"

Instincts propelled Marisa to run, and when she took off, her friends ran with her. That convinced the passengers in the car that she was indeed Mary, and they pursued. It was a crazy scene, saved by a one-way street and a store with a back exit. No one wanted to repeat it.

Ginny, who lived across the street from Colleen when they were young, had been a friend of the twins from the time they were toddlers. When they were little, Sheila and Colleen played together one day, and fought the next day. On those alternate fighting-days, they drove Ginny and each other crazy by pretending to make her their new best friend. After Sheila's death, Colleen and Ginny didn't see much of each other.

Now, they were excited to catch up on personal information again, but their re-connection, though sincere, was never more than an enthusiastic reunion and exchange of numbers leading to nothing.

When Marisa went to the lady's room, Ginny leaned close to say, "You won't believe it, but she's fallen for an OC. We're here to meet him."

"No way," said Colleen.

Two familiar hands covered her eyes, and Wilson whispered something French.

"Want to meet my friends?" Colleen asked him, as she held one of his hands and spread her arm to include the others at the table.

At that moment, Marisa returned. "You two know each other?" she asked.

"We're old friends," Wilson said.

Silence from Marisa.

Colleen understood. She turned to the door.

"We have got to go. Chris and I have to get back to the hospital before the end of visiting hours. Bye, everyone."

She was almost out the door before Christine caught up. At the car she asked, "What visiting hours?"

"I had to get out of there," Colleen answered.

"Why? I don't get it."

"I don't either," Colleen replied.

The next day Wilson called to ask, "Did you make it to visiting hours on time?"

"I beg your pardon?" she said.

"When you had to leave The Tavern to go to the hospital, did you get there in time?"

"Oh. Yes, I did," she answered.

"What about us? When is our visit? How about Saturday afternoon?"

This time he had no car. She bought donuts and coffee and picked him up. They drove around the Ocean Drive and stopped to watch the cormorants catch their dinner. He told her he was being sent to Defense Language School in Monterey to prepare for a swift boat assignment. He gave her his address, they walked on the rocks a little, and he blew her a goodbye kiss when she dropped him off.

Somehow she knew she would never see him again.

Later, after her cousin Christine saw Marisa, Colleen learned Wilson had been killed in Vietnam six weeks after he arrived.

Colleen and Keith had started a correspondence that ramped up as time went by. They became closer friends. He invited her to attend the military ball in Newport with him on New Year's Eve. She had never been to a formal dance at the castle on Ocean Drive. One of the ladies her mother worked for offered to let Colleen use the ball gown from her daughter's debut to New York society. Colleen was walking, but her feet were not touching the ground!

New Year's Eve was enchanting—a bold, crisp moon, the castle decorated like something from a Disney movie, and Keith in full-dress uniform, like Cinderella's prince. They drank champagne and twirled, eating strawberries and chocolates.

When the music stopped, they sat together on a velvet chaise. Keith said, "I don't want to take you home. Let's stay here."

"My mother says I can't do that because we're not married."

"So what?" Keith said. "Let's get hitched! I've been asking you for a long time."

"I didn't think you were serious."

He reached down and touched her foot.

"What's wrong?" she asked.

"I was afraid your feet might be cold," he replied.

"Of course my feet are freezing in these sandals."

He said, "I can take care of that."

And he did.

They made arrangements to marry at the Naval Chapel in Newport. Colleen had a local photographer take her picture in her wedding dress, to be delivered to the *Daily News* for publication on their wedding day. Everywhere she went, people asked if she was nervous.

She wasn't. Not until the day before the wedding when Keith arrived. She met him at the door, barefoot. His face lost its smile.

"What's wrong?" she asked.

"I'm sorry."

"What's the matter?"

"I can't do it."

"Can't get married? Okay. Let's not. I'll call everyone tonight."

"I'd like to talk about this," he said.

"I think we just did."

"Colleen, I'm so sorry. I just can't go forward feeling the way I feel."

She was crying now. "Don't worry. I don't want to, either."

"I wish I could explain it."

"I wish you would leave."

Keith went to the car and she followed him. Colleen opened the trunk to take back the suitcase she'd packed for the honeymoon. She didn't know what possessed her, but she lifted out his locked briefcase.

"Colleen. Stop. What do you think you're doing?"

She took the tire iron and whacked the clasps until they sprang open, spilling photographs and a satin peekaboo shoe on her driveway.

Ending the wedding before its execution took more out of her than she expected. Her anger was beyond any emotion she had ever experienced. She wanted to hurt him. Many ideas crossed her mind. She wanted to hide in the back seat of his car and beat his head beyond recognition before torching the car with a bottle rocket. She wanted the opportunity to finish him off as he choked on a piece of food, or was run over by a bus, or hit by lightning, or buried in a mudslide, or had a heart attack, or a stroke, or was struck by frozen waste jettisoned from an airplane, or fell down an elevator shaft, or was pushed into the path of a train, or got Legionnaire's Disease from a hotel air conditioner, or closed the garage door and was overcome by carbon monoxide, or was struck by a speeding truck while changing a flat on the side of the highway in the rain, or was accidentally shot by a deer hunter, or was beaten to death by a drug addict who went to the wrong house to buy heroin, or was the victim of spontaneous combustion in his Barco-lounger, or was bitten by a rabid bat, or was kidnapped by medical outlaws harvesting organs for experiments and thrown into a vat of sulfur, or fell out of a roller coaster, or was run over by his own car when the emergency brake failed on a steep driveway, or drowned when his car fell off a ferry, or was dragged out to sea by a shark while swimming, or was squished in a warehouse when a pallet of industrial air conditioners fell onto his head, or sleep-walked into the path of an eighteen wheeler, or was dragged off a golf course by a sixteen-foot alligator, or was crushed when a piano fell off a scaffolding, or was speared by kabobs which ricocheted off an exploding gas grill, or was pulled into a cage by a lion, or was overcome by paint fumes, or fell asleep while his body was drained during a blood donation drive, or was eaten by a killer whale while looking into an ice-fishing hole, or was electrocuted by his umbrella in a thunderstorm, or was trampled by a circus elephant checking his pockets for peanuts, or drowned while bobbing for apples on Halloween, or strangled on an escalator when he bent down to tie his shoe and the drawstring from the neck of his jacket was caught in the gears, or slipped on someone's spit at a ball game and landed on his head in the dugout, or fell out of a helicopter touring the Grand Canyon, or was crushed by a wide load on the highway when one of his caustic farts caused him to black out and lose control of his car in a heavy traffic merge, or whatever untoward thing occurred... in the unlikely event it did.

At the end of that long day Colleen did not care why he had cold feet. It made no difference at all to her. She could never forget or forgive it. She knew that much about herself, without the shadow of a doubt.

She had also consumed a great deal of wine, and had cried a gallon of tears. Finally, she couldn't keep her eyes open, and she fell asleep.

Her childhood dreams, like a pile of old coats in a closet during the daylight, would no longer become bogeymen at night. One by one, they disappeared.

A foghorn blasted close. Her father might have stayed at sea, curled up in the wheelhouse hoping a large ship didn't run over his boat and sink him while he waited for the sun to burn the fog off in the morning. Or he could be drunk someplace while her mother worked late. When the answering horn didn't blow, she knew she was in a dream.

In the dream she wanted to know what time it was. The clock was in her parents' room, but she didn't get up to check it. No one knew how scared she was lying in the dark waiting for morning. If she had a clock, she would watch it until four a.m., because, according to the newspaper, most crimes happen between midnight and four a.m.

When Sheila was alive, Colleen listened to her sister's breathing and climbed onto her bed, careful not to wake her. Sheila was a deep sleeper who became loud, fussy and hard to settle down if she was awakened. Their mother had a fit if Colleen woke her up, and the wrath was immediate.

Curling up across the bottom of Sheila's bed, near her feet, generally went unnoticed until dawn. Then, if she was lucky, she could sneak back into her own bed in complete silence. If her mother heard even a floorboard squeak, she would storm into the room. Once, when she was caught tip-toeing around in the middle of the night, Marie demanded to know what scared her.

Colleen's anxiety swirled around like the many-headed Hydra. She was afraid her father would die alone in the fog or that he was drunk someplace and had spent all their money. It scared her to know that an invisible Jesus Christ watched her; she was sure she wasn't good enough. And she missed Sheila everywhere, every day, and wanted to curl up in the bed that still smelled like her sister and never get up. Once, during the time when she couldn't speak, she pointed to a horror comic book.

Her mother opened the scary book.

"Show me what bothers you, *show me!*" Marie insisted.

Colleen pointed to a coffin with a chalk-colored dead man rising from it to pursue screaming mourners. Marie put her arm around Colleen and tightly held her chin with one hand. With her other hand she held the picture in front of her. Colleen struggled to turn away, and cried, but Marie would not let her go. Nights had been terrifying before Sheila died; afterwards, they were worse.

There was that chime again. It wasn't a foghorn or the bell from a buoy, it was a seven-day clock she had bought at an antique barn. She planned to put it on the mantel she would have someday when she was married. Now she had no place for it.

Colleen breathed deep and pulled the covers up. The world was full of people who woke up in the middle of a dream. She wasn't a scared child anymore, she was alone, afraid... adult... and broke. There were the unnecessary invitations, useless dress, the photographer's picture, and a tweed going-away suit waiting at her house for a day that would never arrive. The clothes couldn't be returned; the dress had been worn at fashion shows and was a clearance item; the suit was a final mark-down. It was time to hunker down and make enough money for school. Again. Crap!

It seemed as if Marie would never stop talking about the break-up. Pain and disappointment were a scab she liked to touch. Her comments had a circular pattern—lovers' quarrels and reconciliation.

The theme was "Forgiveness is divine, Christ forgave his killers, certainly there is nothing that can happen that cannot be remedied by forgiveness."

Knowing that no amount of information would satisfy her mother, Colleen gave her none. Besides, what could she say? The whole situation was humiliating. Words were too hard to form.

Colleen sent a note to Louise, her old neighbor from Grove Hall who brought the "Summer with Shakespeare" program to her attention. She might as well find out about that again. And she saw an interesting advertisement in the URI campus rag... the Psych department was offering free group therapy for "Women Left at the Altar." Colleen wrote down the date.

On the appointed evening she joined four women in a meeting room, just to see what she could learn. It was an eye-opening experience. She was surprised to see the women were young and attractive. One was beautiful, but still could not pry her partner away from his obsession. Common problems were horses, hookers, beer, and drugs. After sitting in a circle and saying the serenity prayer, they were instructed to introduce themselves by first name only. Florence, the group leader, had no information that was helpful in assuaging Colleen's anger. She was stuck in loathing and hating, not yet over wanting to hurt Keith. In truth, her feelings scared her; they came from a place so deep, she didn't know it existed.

Worst of all, Colleen couldn't fix the problem. *He* didn't pretend to be someone he wasn't... *she* pretended he was someone he wasn't... and *she* was the one who pretended he wanted to marry her and take care of her. No one should have to *pretend* to want to be married just to please her.

The facilitator addressed Colleen, "Are you married, dear?"

"No. We broke our engagement three weeks before the wedding." Colleen started to cry.

"Probably the best thing that ever happened to you," said Kelly. She was a tall shapely blonde who had modeled hosiery and nightgowns for the Sears catalogue, now in the midst of her second divorce. Her last husband lost all interest in her after he started to travel on business trips with a co-worker who had been a massage therapist in a previous life.

Florence said God might be sending Colleen a message by revealing a problem that needed to be addressed before her holy vows.

Amy completed the circle. A natural blonde with a fresh healthy glow, flawless skin, and a brilliant smile, she had the clear blue eyes of her Scandinavian heritage, but her brightness faded when she spoke of Bernard, her husband who complained she was too big, too Caucasian, and looked too much like a California girl. He suggested she get a tattoo to make herself more interesting. Amy was horrified.

At Christmas he gave her a gift certificate for a tattoo. She selected one for her foot. When she finally she got it, Bernard was elated and their relationship intensified, albeit only temporarily. Soon he was tired of her again and resumed his complaints. Her spying confirmed that he had a girlfriend, although he denied it. And in spite of the fact that it disgusted her, she was having an affair herself, because she wanted to get even.

She was at the end of her rope and had no idea why she had married him. He was a miserable person and so was she. Nothing made any sense. That's why she came to the group. She took a sip from a thermos of coffee mixed with vodka.

Florence said, "Will you stay and talk with me after the group goes home, Amy?"

"I can't," Amy said. "Maybe next time." She took another drink from the thermos.

Florence told the women that the quest for satisfaction is the basis for all addictions.

When one addiction is overcome, it is frequently replaced by another. The women were warned to expect relapses, and to be alert for triggers. Florence said they would find their observations useful in future meetings when they discussed relapse-prevention strategies. She also pointed out that men think the perfect wife will give them the satisfaction they seek, long for, dream of, imagine, create false memories of, and lie about. They lie not only to others, but to themselves.

Colleen was still too angry to have a normal conversation. Thankfully, no one expected small talk.

A few nights later, she had a dream that gave her some relief. She found herself in a beautiful meditation garden that was quiet and cool. A feeling of peace calmed her. She was wearing a dark trench coat and carried a large black purse containing an umbrella and a hammer. It had been raining when she left for work, and she wore black slacks and a black sweater under the trench coat.

On the way home she drove by an old meditation spot similar to the one in her dream. Sitting in the quiet of the tranquility garden, she prayed for help. When she felt better, she left.

Colleen was so sick of moping around, that when a few of the old high school crowd asked her to join them on Sunday afternoon at Hurley's, a jazz bar in Newport, she agreed. The music was a welcome change from work and school, and she hadn't ventured out in a month. At a corner table the girls indulged in people watching. The jazz buffs were interesting and random musicians showed up with their instruments to jam with the regular group.

As time went by and the crowd increased, there were no places to sit. Several newcomers asked if they could take the extra seats at the girls' table. One put his hand out and said, "Hi Colleen, I'm John Winkworth."

Colleen shook his hand. "How do you know my name?"

"I looked at your picture everyday for months when I was at the Defense Language School in Monterey. It was a candid shot at a football game and you stood out in front of a crowd, wearing a different color than everyone else. I never forget a face."

"I remember the day. I was sorry to hear about Wilson's death."

"Oh, it seemed worse than it was, you know how head wounds can be... a lot of blood. But he's okay now."

"I thought he was dead."

"Wounded. Shot on the side of his head, took a piece of his ear and a little of his head, he dove out of the boat and it saved his life but gave him a nasty infection," John explained. Then he added, "I thought you were married."

"No."

"Divorced?" he asked.

"No," she answered. "Why?"

"He's a close friend of mine. He told me that when he was sent back from Vietnam, he went to your house, and your mother told him you were married and living in California."

Colleen said, "You must be mistaken. My family moved out of Newport. He wouldn't have known where to find them."

"Well, I don't know about that, but I heard you were married and living in California. Interesting."

"And I heard he was killed in Vietnam," Colleen said.

"The first reports of his wounds were 'exaggerated,' as they say."

When Colleen got up to leave, John asked for her phone number. He said he wanted to give it to Wilson the next time they spoke.

That night Colleen said, "Mom, did Wilson come to our house asking for me last year?"

There was a strange hesitation before Marie said, "I don't remember anything like that."

"You don't sound sure."

"I'm pretty sure. Why?"

Colleen knew her mother was lying. She had been found out, and now wouldn't admit it. "I met one of his friends today and he told me that you said I was married and living in California."

"It probably was before the wedding that was going to happen and didn't happen. I might have said you were going to get married and live in California. He must have misunderstood."

"Right. I don't appreciate that, Mom. And I don't think you'd like it if I took it upon myself to lie to your friends about you. Maybe you should mind your own business."

"I'm sorry, Colleen. I just don't remember. But I'm sorry."

"I'm sorry too, Mom. And I don't believe you."

The next night Wilson called.

"So your mother must really dislike me. I went to your house but had no luck. Your neighbor gave me your new address in Portsmouth, and I went there. Your mother was very happy to tell me you were married."

"She says she doesn't remember."

"How old is she?"

"Old enough to know better."

They both laughed.

"What about your death by sniper fire?"

"I dove out of the boat and into the river when the shooting started. One bullet grazed my head and resulted in a lot of blood, another got me in a vital organ—the rear-end."

"I don't know what to say. Maybe congratulations."

"Colleen, there's something I have to talk to you about. It's not a big deal and I know it will be fine when you understand, but you have to promise not to hang up."

"I promise," she answered.

"I'm married," he said. "We don't live together, and..."

Colleen put her hand on the counter next to her mother's scissors. She softly put the phone down and cut the cord.

Louise still worked in the administration office at U of Florida. She had processed Colleen's request to be readmitted and was able to assure her that the credits from URI were accepted. She had also resurrected her exchange student status for nine hours of Shakespeare at Cambridge, including the financial aid and transportation. If her whole world hadn't been falling apart, Colleen would have been ecstatic. One thing was certain—going to England was just what she needed. Going to Bora Bora would have been better, or the moon, even... but Cambridge was a good substitute.

It rained hard on the day before she was supposed to leave. In the coziness of the car, driving through the pounding deluge, she reflected on the fact that the statues in the old meditation garden were nice. They looked like real people, only stronger.

On her way home after an exhausting day at work, she drove by the garden again. She parked the car under the same huge tree, close to the road. Her large black bag was still in the trunk and it still contained her umbrella and the hammer. Bringing it with her, she sat in the quiet of the empty garden and prayed for guidance. For a long time, she had been putting one foot in front of the other. Now she needed direction. She needed help. Advancing quietly toward one of the garden statues, she observed its beautiful bare feet, and thought about Keith and his foot fetish. She raised the hammer.

Swinging as hard as she could, she hacked left and right, down and up, and down again. Breathless and splattered with bits of plaster and powder, she moved to the corner where another statue waited. Soon pieces of pale feet littered the lawn. Whacked and chopped and shattered chunks of toes and heels became rubble that could never be feet again.

On her way back to the car she noticed St. Francis in the garden. He was sturdier than the others, and had only one concrete foot poking out from under his robe. But Colleen was worn out. St. Francis was safe.

On the way home, pounding rain bounced off the roof like a thousand spears. The throbbing noise drummed out all other sound. The next morning, she went to the airport.

13 CAMBRIDGE

At the airport in New York, Colleen waited beside a lone peacenik girl wearing a cowboy hat, and dragging a heavy backpack and a guitar case. They chatted briefly about the Jazz Festival in Newport, and The Blue Onion, a small coffee house on Thames Street where folk singers performed.

When the peacenik took her hat off and said, "My name is Amberjean," Colleen dropped her suitcase.

"What? Amberjean Frazier from Attleboro, Mass?" Colleen squealed. "Amberjean who used to call her grandparents 'Ammadaa' and 'PaMa'? Cousin Adeline's little Amberjean, all grown up?"

The girls hugged each other and leaned back, still holding hands. It was an unbelievable moment. They could have been sisters.

Sure, Colleen was older, but they both had long chestnut hair, pale freckles, rosy cheeks, and great big smiles. They were the same height, and looked like they had dressed in the same closet. They leaned in to each other like family members who delighted in each other's company. When they found out they were on the same flight, they arranged to sit together.

They flew on the Super Connie, a behemoth with four props that carried 102 passengers and was heavier and larger than the regular Constellation. They talked from take-off until landing. The wind was so strong in Newfoundland, where they refueled, that they walked to the station in groups of eight, holding each other for fear of being blown away. Arm in arm, they found their luggage after the flight, and they took the train to Cambridge together.

When her mother worked at the hospital, Amberjean had lived in Newport, and her fondest childhood memories were associated with Mrs. Benson, Jamestown Ferry rides, and everything Newport.

In Cambridge, she was meeting two of her musician friends to perform at schools for the deaf in England and Ireland. They planned to add to their repertoire of songs protesting war and injustice, while they worked on new material and encouraged young musicians. For a moment Colleen envied the trip Amberjean described. But that was before she saw Cambridge.

Odd-looking iron contraptions, used as bike rests, were attached to boulders arranged in circles around huge old trees in ancient cobblestone courtyards. "Who has been here before me?" Colleen wondered. "If bicycles were new in 1840, and these trees are over three hundred years old, whose ghost is sitting on this rock with me, right now?" Elderly people, who looked like they had been around since the invention of the wheel, rode ancient bikes.

One of Colleen's professors waved as he breezed by with his pants tucked inside his socks, secured with a rubber band. Women rode while wearing heels, and used scarves to secure their hats. They pulled their skirts up away from the gears and held them on the handlebars, oblivious to the spectacle they created. Many schlepped groceries in baskets attached to the front handlebars and hanging off the sides of the back fender. It seemed odd that they were not splattered all over the street, considering the amount of flapping fabric near spinning wheels.

One day it rained nearly all day, heavy and quiet, stopping and starting so silently and often that she ignored it. After she realized that she had left her umbrella in one of her classes, Colleen set off to check the lost and found. She went to find the main gatehouse entrance where the gatekeeper was.

The porter was a watchman for the courtyard although most of the time the doors were wide open and so were the windows. There were apparently no screens in England. Colleen asked if there was a lost and found and if anyone had turned in an umbrella.

"No," he said.

In the background, a slight man in a blue jumpsuit popped up. "Wait, darlin'. Come with me." The small man turned and walked quickly into the rain as Colleen raced to catch up. There was no conversation. Before he darted into one of the buildings he spoke over his shoulder, "Down here, luv."

Down and down, they went until a sign pointing to a hallway said, "Ladies Toilet." He opened the door and went in. She followed the little man through another door at the end of the bathroom, to enter a storeroom. There they were… umbrellas stacked everywhere, an elephants' graveyard of umbrellas.

"What color do you like, luv? I find at least one a day. I bring them all here, and if someone wants one, I give one back."

Colleen took a blue one. The one she had lost was black with white spots, but she liked this one better, and she took good care of it.

One of the international students, Vincenzio, was a young Italian who had been paralyzed in a diving accident. While not rich, he managed to support himself with his settlement. He loved to travel and took teaching jobs all over the world. After completing his present course, he had a contract to teach English in Finland.

Handsome and well built, he looked like a movie star pretending to be handicapped; he had braces on his legs and metal canes with handles that encircled his wrists. Although he had explained his impediment and requested lodging on the first floor, his room was on the third floor and none of the buildings had elevators. When his application for a room re-assignment was denied, he didn't complain, but spent his spare time looking for shortcuts so he could be on time for class.

Slow around campus, Vincenzio was always one of the first at the pub. If Amberjean wasn't playing out of town, she visited Colleen and broke in her new songs at the campus bar. Vincenzio eagerly waved them over. He loved it when both cousins showed up.

One brisk evening when Amberjean was back in town, Colleen talked her into attending one of her required plenary lectures. Like members of an ancient tribe returning to the safety of the campfire, they clutched their wraps and leaned into the wind on their way to the lecture hall. A Don of Medieval Studies and author of a linguistic dictionary recited an Icelandic saga in Middle English.

The lecture was ninety minutes without a break, and bore only a tangential relationship to the regular curriculum. The professor noted that the Icelandic people still preferred to get their history the way they did before writing—they liked to hear it.

Since the Middle Ages, each family that settled in Iceland could be traced to modern times, and every family member was known by name. The professor's saga, recited entirely without notes, was a series of elaborate grunts and guttural noises. Even though he did not say one recognizable word, the hall was silent with spellbound students. At the end, they clapped and the Don walked out without a glance. Colleen had understood it all in some primitive way, and was profoundly moved. She wasn't the only one. As she turned to go, she noticed Amberjean wiping tears from her eyes.

If it had been daytime, the lecture hall doorway and steps would have been crowded with students discussing their thoughts on what they had heard. Tonight, everyone went to the campus pub.

Bypassing a group that was arguing about the relevance of devoting a lifetime to learning a language that was almost dead, they joined a group discussing the importance of an exceptional teacher, such as the one they had just heard. Several decided, on the spot, to change their major to medieval studies.

Then tables and chairs were pushed aside, and Amberjean took a seat at the piano. She played the vamp for "I Feel Good," by James Brown, and the standing crowd clapped to the strong beat. Soon they formed a large circle, and each took a turn in the center. Even John, singing while he served beer, came from behind the bar to dance. The girls were hoarse by the time the night ended.

"It's so late. Why don't you stay at my place?" Colleen asked. "The couch is comfortable, and tomorrow morning we can have a really fabulous breakfast." As far as Colleen was concerned, Cambridge was best in the morning. Breakfast was a feast fit for King Henry on his way to a hunt. There were eggs cooked to order, porridge, beans, tomatoes cut in half and broiled, pastries, string bacon (which was yucky, regular bacon almost completely uncooked, "string" referring to the little lines of meat in the fat), and the *piéce de la resistance*, fried bread… thick white bread, buttered on both sides and fried in deep fat. On a scale of one to ten, Colleen rated it a twelve.

The next day, Vincenzio decided it was easier for him to drink in his room, than to drag his legs home after a party in the pub, so he invited everyone to a party in his room after their last class. He called it, *l'ora dell'apperativo*.

He said he had little in the way of refreshments, but he promised to make sangria. Colleen took a quick jog to the store to buy cheese and crackers. Amberjean arrived with her guitar and a bottle of rum, and buddies from class and the regular crowd from the pub brought Coca-Cola, a bag of pistachios, a whole salami, and a bong.

Vincenzio's room was a large single with a piano that was located at the top of the stairs, across from the bathroom, in the very center of traffic. He left the door open and invited passersby to come in and play a song on the piano to give Amberjean a break, so that she could play her guitar. A cup of sangria inspired many to belt out tunes they learned as children. The music and the impromptu gathering were an amazing success.

The buildings were ancient and hot. A window fan and a candle on top of the piano were all they had to keep themselves cool… it didn't help with the temperature, but it added to the atmosphere. It was a good-humored crowd that trooped down the stairs and over to the dining hall when the sangria was gone.

No sooner had they taken their seats than the power failed, leaving only table candles to light the cavernous hall. Dinner wine made the group more buoyant as the meal progressed. Later, they could see that the whole campus was dark, and it was impossible to study. On the edge of boisterous, and ready to celebrate almost anything, they ambled down the sidewalk to the campus pub, which was also without power.

The bartenders were standing on the steps because the beer taps were inoperable. Students joined them, creating a large thirsty crowd. By now the *ora dell'apperativo*, the dinner wine, and the lack of electricity, had left many feeling the call of the wild.

Amberjean asked John, the bartender, if he knew where Lord Byron's pool was.

"I do, and I'll take you," he said.

"How many can you take?" She glanced at the crowd. "Three?"

"Okay, three."

John negotiated his absence with the other bartenders and biked home to get the Mini Cooper while four women and Vincenzio went to the street to wait. They decided to flip a coin to see who would go. It wasn't dark yet, but deep dusk, a magic hour.

Out of nowhere, John drove up in a battered VW bus with a wheelchair attached by bungee cord to the luggage rack. "My brother brought my Mum for the weekend, and I let him talk me into trading this for the Mini. He promised to buy petrol for the mini if I would take the van. The old bloke's got a bird."

There was room for all of them, with Vincenzio in front next to John. Off they went through the fairy tale countryside to Grandchester Village. John made a sharp turn onto an unmarked dirt road and stopped at a small car park. Nothing identified the place, but everyone got out, and John turned to Vincenzio. "My mum said you could use her chair if you don't get it wet." They both laughed.

In a moment he had it off the roof, and snapped it open. Vincenzio leaned so far back in it that they all held their breath afraid the chair would fall over, or he would fall out. Instead, he *twirled!* The canes from his wrists were beside him on the seat! Everyone was speechless.

John pointed to the woods. "Follow that path. I'll be back in an hour or so."

They took off down the hard-packed dirt path. Vincenzio's upper body strength made him fast in the chair. "Passing on the left," he announced as he made beeping noises, and overtook the others... laughing louder than anyone.

When a jogger ran by, startling them in the almost-dark, one of them yelled, "Where is Lord Byron's pool?"

"Keep going," he said over his shoulder.

"How far?" they yelled.

"Not far," the runner said, and disappeared.

They walked beside a narrow, scummy river, where swans and ducks returned their gaze.

The splashing sound of a small waterfall indicated the edge of a marble dam that slowed the water and created a wide area nearby... a natural pool. They stood around it and someone said, "This is it. I've been here before."

They gathered near a small bench and a plaque on a wooden post, the first marker that identified the spot as Lord Byron's Pool.

Suddenly they were all giddy because the water, the moonlight, and the alcohol, made it seem like Lord Byron was present. Vincenzio went straight to the edge. Amberjean joined Colleen on the bench. Someone said, "Let's jump in." And they started to talk about whether to take off all their clothes. Most wanted to, but some didn't.

During this time, no one noticed Vincenzio struggling out of his shirt and pants, and dropping them beside the wheelchair. He reached down and folded the footrests up, placing his feet over the edge of the grass, dangling them just above the water. He was perched on the edge of the seat.

Suddenly Sandy shouted, "Look! Vincenzio is naked!" At that very moment, he used his arms to pull himself up and push off, launching his whole body into the water. The air was full of screams and laughter. They had most of their clothes off when Vincenzio surfaced and swam strongly away. "It's great," he said. "Come join me."

They jumped in one after the other.

The "pool" was about eight feet deep everywhere. Colleen had jumped in right at the edge, and the lack of steps or handholds made her wonder how they would ever get Vincenzio out. If all else failed, maybe when John returned, he could drive the van up the path and throw them a rope tied to the bumper. In the meantime, the moon was bright, and the water was black, and they felt like wild young forest creatures; their splashes released an unworldly phosphorescence.

After a little while, they wanted to get out. Sandy, the strongest, went first. She had no problem. Then she held the hand of another girl and helped her walk up the rock-hard earth on the side. Together they helped the next, each holding a hand. Two of the women already out of the water helped the next one, and then it was Vincenzio's turn. Amberjean and Sandy made a sling with a pair of jeans and told him to sit in it, with his back toward them. They pulled him straight up and over the edge of the bank, sitting him on the grass.

They named themselves *The Lord Byron Swim Team,* and when someone suggested that they all throw their underpants to the Gods of the pool to memorialize the evening, they howled like wolves. Even Vincenzio threw his. Walking back through the woods, it was so dark under the trees that they had to look up at the sky to stay on the path.

Before long, John arrived to pick them up.

Back at campus, the lights were still out, the pub was still closed, and they were so tired they called it a day. Amberjean stayed over again.

On the way to her room, Colleen checked the mail and found a letter from home.

Dear Colleen,

I haven't had time to write before now, but I wanted to dash this off while I had a minute. I have been having indigestion and vertigo. What's new with you?

There was a case of vandalism in Philomena Meditation Garden. Someone attacked a lot of statues. It was in the paper. I think it happened after you left, but I'm enclosing an article from today's news. As you can see, Keith is raising money to repair the damage. He looks good in the picture, don't you think? I don't know if you keep in touch, but if you do, I thought you might want to compliment him on his civic mindedness. I always thought he had a nice way about him. And remember, you didn't learn to hold a grudge from me.

Your father backed into a car at a stop sign last night. You know how he always puts the car in neutral coming down hills and at stoplights to save gas. Well, he was on his way back from the Home Brew and at a four-way stop sign. He got mixed up, thinking it was a stoplight. When he started, he put it in reverse instead of first, a simple mistake. When he got out of the car, the other driver was very rude and called him a drunk. I don't know what we are going to do. That man wants money to fix the front of his car and your father says it wasn't his fault. We don't have money to fix anyone's car, including ours. Everyone gets confused sometimes. The man is just trying to take advantage of your father because he's old. I wasn't home, it was my bingo night. I go to the doctor tomorrow, and if they want to operate, I'm going to let them. I'm so sick of feeling this way, I'll try anything.

Keep having a good time. Life changes before you know it, and you will become old and no one will want you, or care how bad you feel.

Love, Mom

Colleen looked at the newspaper clipping.

"I wish I had a letter from my mom," Amberjean said. "I miss her as much now as I did the day she died."

When they reached her room, Colleen replied, "I'll share with you." She handed the envelope to Amberjean and headed down the hall with her toothbrush and pajamas.

When Colleen returned, Amberjean said, "How about Keith and those statues?"

"Mmmm," Colleen answered.

"He's really good looking," Amberjean observed, looking at the newspaper.

"Yup," said Colleen.

"And that's a good thing he's doing, but of all the charities and worthwhile causes out there, how did he get interested in vandalized statues? I don't get it."

"I know," Colleen responded.

"Do you miss him?"

Colleen's eyes were full. "He was my best friend. I miss him a lot. But in the end, he wasn't honest and he wasn't my friend. There is no changing that."

Amberjean took a watch out of her pocket and looked at the time. "I'm so beat, I'd better turn in. I hope there are no ghosts here."

"I know," Colleen answered, "This place must be full of them."

"My dog, Agatha, visited recently," said Amberjean.

"Tell me about her."

Amberjean said she thought she loved Agatha too much. Even though her grandparents would have welcomed more dogs, she was afraid Agatha wouldn't like it.

She said, "Dogs are pack animals removed from their families soon after birth to spend a lonely lifetime with a different species. They give unconditional love and accept their owner as their leader because they must. Their very life depends upon the pleasure of someone from a different species."

Amberjean had looked into Agatha's eyes and knew this was true. Agatha trembled in her sleep and barked of her sacrifices. When she spoke in Amberjean's dreams, her voice wasn't human. It had a hollow sound, like someone who has lost her larynx and holds a finger in front of her tracheotomy hole while breathing words. When Amberjean heard the strange voice, she simultaneously felt Agatha's fur, softer than cashmere.

They had been very close. When Amberjean left the house, Agatha lay by the big window and waited. When she took care of her grandmother with cancer, Agatha lay by the bed and watched. When Agatha got cancer, Amberjean had her euthanized.

On the day of Agatha's appointment, she seemed better. The vet said, "It's often like this. They seem to know, and all of a sudden they act like they're getting well. Do you want to wait another day?"

"No," she said.

Agatha's vet bill was huge. How many things had she done in a lifetime that troubled her? Not many. But this one never left. It adhered to the pericardium lining her heart, existing in the synapses between the axons that fueled her brain.

For a while she was a frequent visitor to dog pounds, bringing treats, walking the aisles, looking in cages. But her eyes never met any canine eyes that looked back with interest... maybe they all knew about Agatha.

She encouraged other people to adopt a dog and sometimes she helped them find one. Her friends considered her an expert at matching an animal with a family, noting to each other that it was strange that she couldn't find a pet for herself, when she so obviously wanted one.

Amberjean had said too much. To change the subject, she said, "Tell me about your ghost."

Colleen looked away. "You know, my twin, Sheila, always did as she was told. I did not. I constantly goaded her to use our language. I was stubborn. I constantly goaded her to disobey until she started to fight with me. We were pushing each other one morning on my father's boat when Sheila accidentally stepped in a rope, went over the side, and drowned. When she visits me, which doesn't happen often anymore, she always speaks our twin talk."

Amberjean said, "Would you say something to me in your language?"

"I don't really remember it when I'm awake," said Colleen.

"What did you talk about?" Amberjean asked.

"It was more like soothing sounds that meant, 'Good night, I love you'," said Colleen. "We used to be in the same crib. We soothed and comforted each other a lot when we were really little."

"That must have been wonderful," Amberjean said.

"It was unbelievably wonderful."

Amberjean was asleep before the courtyard clock finished chiming.

In the quiet of the dark, Colleen's thoughts turned to Sheila. They were supposed to be taking a nap. Sheila was quiet and content, fast asleep. Colleen, with tears still falling, watched the leaves twisting in the sun outside their bedroom window and listened to her sister's soft breathing.

They had been playing hide-and-seek in the yard and wore the brand-new, yellow angora sweaters that Marie knitted. Colleen ran between two bushes right into a huge spider web that fell on her like a tent. It covered her hair, face, and clothes all the way to her waist. Suddenly the angora felt as sticky as the spider web and she thought that spiders were crawling all over her. She became frantic.

Sheila laughed instead of helping her get out of the stickiness and the bugs. At home their mother made light of her tears and wiped the web off the sweater. When Colleen refused to wear it again, Marie was furious. But neither bribe nor threat could ever convince her to touch it again.

Sometimes to trick her, Sheila put that angora sweater in her drawer under other clothes. Colleen screamed when her hand accidentally brushed against its furriness, and Marie descended on her as though her knitting had been intentionally insulted.

Remembering her magical swim in Lord Byron's Pool, and the clear-black water splashed with phosphorescence, Colleen smiled. In daylight she probably would have seen scum and dirt and swan poop.

"Mom," she thought. "I hope you've noticed that I've grown up, and if you can find that yellow angora sweater, I'll wear it now." She curled into the pillow and slept. It was late morning before noise from outside woke them up.

14 Wilson

While Amberjean was singing, Wilson slid into the booth beside Colleen, and said, "*Tu es magnifique.*"

"*Qu'est-ce qui t'a pris autant de temps?*" (What took you so long?), she whispered in return.

He laughed and put his briefcase on the table.

She couldn't believe those words had just come from her mouth. Ignoring their import, she quickly changed the subject. "How did you find me?"

"I can't reveal my sources."

"Why are you here, Wilson?"

"To finish the conversation we were having when you so callously hung up on me. I want to show you some pictures." He reached for the case.

"Hold it," she said. "How did you find me?"

"I had a hunch you would either have your grades transferred or go back to Gainesville. I called administration and asked for your friend, Louise. She gave me a little help, and then I called Cambridge to check. Being in Naval Intelligence is a little like being a detective."

He opened the briefcase and gave her a small folder. On top was a group shot of his class at the Defense Language School.

"That's Hong, our teacher, in the front on the left. *Hong* means Rose. Vietnamese girls are often named after flowers." He pointed to three young naval officers. "These three guys are dead."

He handed her a picture of himself standing beside a tall, smiling man whose buzz cut was so short, he looked bald.

"Here's Charlie, no mistaking a Marine haircut," he said. "Charlie was in the class ahead of me, but we lived in neighboring rooms, and became close. He wanted to go out with Rose, but she wouldn't go anywhere alone with him. He told her he didn't want to be alone with her anyway, and suggested she bring a friend, another teacher. Rose's friend Lang agreed, and Charlie convinced me to keep Lang company so that he could spend time with Rose. He didn't tell me how old she was. I could have been her son; she was in her mid-forties then. Here, she's in one of these pictures. Take a look."

Colleen's jaw dropped at the middle-aged Vietnamese woman named Lang. "Yikes," she said, "What does Lang mean?"

"Sweet potato," he answered. "I thought I would help Charlie out just once, but it turned out to be more, a lot more. Lang was a language teacher too. Nice lady. Old, but nice. And it's not like I had a lot to do socially.

"When Charlie and Rose decided to get married, he called his family, his friends, everyone he knew. I looked forward to acting as his best man. We were shocked when he was called up and had to leave early to replace a casualty. He left so quickly there was no time to get a marriage license."

Colleen saw a Legal "Marriage by Proxy" form in the folder. Charlie Fairlington, "Groom," was marrying Hong Tran, "Bride," with Michael Wilson as "Proxy."

"It was Charlie's idea," Wilson continued. "He got the form, made sure everyone had signed it, and went to get it notarized. Of course, the notary wanted to check IDs and witness the signatures. Charlie rounded us up and brought us to the bank where the notary was waiting. We signed everything, and had it notarized. It was like a party. Hong, Lang, Charlie, me, several neighbors, and a bunch of Marines, who were already there to celebrate."

"In the confusion, Charlie didn't sign the form. Then he was gone, and Rose found out she was pregnant. The proxy idea had been his, but in the end, it was useless."

"What's this?" Colleen asked.

The next picture showed Wilson at a city hall marriage with a very pregnant Rose. "A lot of things happened," he said.

"Charlie was captured. Rose had problems, and rather than let her get caught up in red tape and risk the baby's health, or death, I married her so she could have Charlie's health insurance. That way she and the baby had doctors. We've never lived together. Lang stays with her, which helps with expenses. They both work, and between the two of them, they take care of the baby. His name is True. Rose has been able to handle almost everything. It's just like having the proxy, only without the proxy form."

Colleen looked at Wilson. "Only you."

"What do you think?" he asked.

"I think that if I were explaining this to you, and showing you pictures of my Vietnamese husband, you would be out the door."

"Ask me about my future plans."

"Okay, tell me about your future plans."

"Well. I hope Charlie escapes or is freed. One way or the other, I've done everything I can for him by helping Rose and True. And because Rose and I don't live together, we can be divorced after one year of separation. I'll continue to be in the little guy's life, like an uncle, until his real dad arrives. I love him and always will.

"Meanwhile, my grandfather died. I inherited forty thousand dollars, and I've been looking at a farm. I brought some pictures, but I'd like you to come and see it. It's a small piece of heaven. The land is beautiful—eight hundred acres, a small river, a pond, a few simple outbuildings, room to grow and build. There's an old-fashioned small town with a one-room schoolhouse in need of a teacher, if you'd like a job. One of the buildings is a four-room cabin that can be made suitable for True and Rose and Lang, if they'd like to stay there for a while. I can live in the bunkhouse with whoever I get to help me run the place. There is a nice knoll where I can imagine putting a real house someday." He picked up a picture of a pond with a hill behind it and handed it to Colleen.

"And I have a message for you," he said handing her a letter from Rose.

Dear Colleen,

I am so happy Wilson found you. He is man with large heart and big spirit.

When True sees him, he jumps for joy. Marriage saved my life and my son's. I am grateful forever. Our divorce should be quick, OK.

I write a letter to Charlie every day. Every night I pray he receives my letter and see his son, soon. I hope I see you soon too.

Sincerely, Hong Tran

Wilson put his pictures back in his briefcase as Amberjean announced, "My favorite song, the one I close with every night, has a special meaning this evening, and I'm dedicating it to Colleen O'Leary, a member of my family that I have not seen since I was a baby. As a matter of fact, we accidentally found each other at the airport on our way here... I hope everyone will sing along."

She turned up the amps, and the whole pub began to sing, "We Shall Overcome."

Wilson whispered, "I respect your freedom to follow your conscience. But as long as I have a friend who is being force-marched in North Vietnam, I hope you respect my civil obedience."

Later, he continued, "There was a piece in yesterday's *Times* that quotes a Vietcong leader who said that even ten years after the fact, they are still holding French POWs because their physical condition would create negative world opinion. They say they are in the same position with American POWs, that injuries suffered from a crash landing would be attributed to torture, instead of falling out of an airplane. It's best to keep them as prisoners."

"If we weren't sending armed men into their country to attack them, they wouldn't have POWs," Amberjean answered.

"It's late," Colleen said. "We can't resolve this, and we should discuss it another time."

"Fine with me," Wilson said, and changed the subject. "Amberjean, how did you find your way to performing?"

She pulled her hair back and away from her ears. "This had a lot to do with it."

"What happened to your ears?" he asked.

Amberjean said, "I was born without external ears. I spent a lot of time in doctors' offices, and my mother brought books to keep me occupied. One story, about a musical bear, really captivated me. After that, my mother found a how-to-play-the-guitar book, and eventually she bought me a small guitar and a keyboard. My favorite doctor was a guitar player himself, and he helped me enormously.

"At first, I just banged the instruments, but I felt the rhythm of vibrations, and over time, I learned to read music. I got books and records from the library and studied a lot on my own. It kept me busy, and I had plenty of time.

"I started writing songs before I realized what I was doing. I picked words for their syllable count and rhythm. I don't know which came first, the lyrics or the melody, but I hear music even without using my ears. During this time I had a number of surgeries, my ears were constructed, and in the end, my hearing was almost normal. By then music had taken over my life."

"My uncle Padraig—my father's brother—was born without ears," Colleen said.

"I never heard a word about him," Amberjean replied. "Did he sign, or have prosthetics?"

"Neither. They kept him at home. When he was young, sign language was considered against God's plan by many educators," Colleen answered. "Uncle Padraig and my father grew up in Somerset on a small farm. Their land ended at the shoreline, within sight of the Fall River textile mills. Years ago my grandfather ran clambakes for the mill workers, and my father and Uncle Padraig helped."

"Where is your uncle now?" Amberjean asked.

"According to my mother's last letter, he's in an old folk's home and not doing well. We didn't live close, and we rarely saw him." Colleen riffled through her purse in an effort to locate the letter.

"That is really sad," Wilson said.

"I've never met anyone besides myself without ears," replied Amberjean.

They were all tired and ready to turn in. The porter told Wilson he had an empty room available for the weekend, and Amberjean stayed over with Colleen.

"What about your grandparents?" Colleen asked when they were alone. "When they understood that you were serious about going on stage, did they try to discourage you?"

"Actually, my grandparents spoiled me. They may have been surprised, but they didn't object."

"What about your father?"

"No one knows anything about my real father. When my mother was alive, she used to say he was lost in the war. After she died, my grandmother told me my mother had planned to tell me about it when I was older. My grandmother said she didn't know anything about my father, not even his name, and she didn't want to lie to me any longer."

"Wow," Colleen said. "I'm sorry."

"Thanks. But not having a father isn't strange to me. I'm used to it. And I do have a stepfather."

The next morning Colleen made coffee in her room, and they chatted.

Amberjean began, "I almost told you about my ears that night at Lord Byron's Pool. When I put my hair in a ponytail, I was sure you saw them."

Colleen replied, "It must have been too dark. Why do you keep your ears a secret?"

"I don't. I decided not to mention them immediately because I usually do, and that launches a lot of questions. In the end I am frustrated because I've met someone I don't know a thing about, and all I've talked about is my ears. I hate it, yet I'm the one who starts it. I want to become friends the way people normally do. And I wanted to see how long it would take before my ears came up. They must not be as obvious as I thought."

Colleen said, "They're definitely not obvious. If you hadn't pulled your hair back, I still wouldn't know." There was a pause. "What about your stepfather?" Colleen asked. "Do you live with him when you're not traveling?"

"I've never lived with David. Soon after my mother married him, he was sent to Korea. We were going to live with him in Port Hueneme when he came back, but then my mother died, and I stayed with my grandparents at their place in Attleboro. I had already spent most of my life there.

"When my stepfather came back, he was a stranger to me. I didn't want to go with him to California, but he talked me into a visit, to check it out. I guess he thought I didn't have much fun on the farm, which was true. But he was already seeing a lady.

"He said she was just a friend, who was trying to be helpful, but she had a couple of bossy girls, older than me, and I was used to being grandma's pet. Anyway, I told him I wanted to live with my grandparents, and that was fine. I don't remember when it happened, but David is now married to that helpful lady, and those bossy girls run him ragged. Besides, my doctors were in Boston, so staying in Attleboro made sense to everyone."

Colleen said, "Seeing how great you're doing makes me feel awful about how Uncle Padraig was treated fifty-some years ago. Even members of his own family assumed he was retarded because he couldn't communicate. There were no opportunities for him to receive an education or have a normal life.

"Here!" Colleen found her mother's letter and read it aloud.

"Your father's brother Padraig had to be put in a state home for old folks. It was hard to find one that would accept the deaf and dumb. He didn't have any money, so they sold the farm at an auction to pay for his keep. Your father went to see him once, but he won't go again. He says it's too depressing."

Amberjean said, "What a miserable situation."

It was almost time to meet Wilson, and the girls hurried.

Amberjean said, "A group of thirteen former Seabees are meeting in Holly Loch, Scotland, where they built a large project years ago. David's stopping here to see me on the way to that reunion. In fact, he says he has something to give me. Why don't you and Wilson come to lunch with us? We don't usually have much to talk about, and he would enjoy meeting my friends."

Colleen said, "That sounds like a great idea. Are Mama Dot and Pa-Ma still alive?"

Amberjean looked away. "They died a few years ago, on their way to visit my grandfather's brother in upstate New York. I think it was the first time they ever took a vacation. They'd planned it for weeks—Niagara Falls, Saratoga, and his brother's house in Binghampton. A neighbor took care of the animals on the farm. I would have gone along, but I had a commitment to teach guitar at a kids' music camp.

"Anyway, they stopped for lunch, and getting back on the interstate, they were hit by a tractor trailer. They both died instantly. David was named executor of their will, and everything was left to me. After selling the farm, he put the proceeds into a trust account. I'm not rich, but I get a monthly check. It means I can follow my heart and share my love of music with deaf children and still afford to live and buy food. I'll never be rich or famous, but I'm able to support myself doing what I love, and I'm happy."

Colleen was shaken. "Good God, Amberjean. Your family is almost gone."

Amberjean paused. "It shook me up pretty bad. But I've met a lot of wonderful people who include me in their families."

Colleen said, "I know what you mean. I think of my friends as family... my chosen family. But still..."

The day started slow. Amberjean had planned to meet her stepfather at the train station. She said, "Colleen, why don't I take him to The Anchor for a late lunch? That way, we can sit outside and watch the river punts. If he wants to spend the extra time, we can take a boat ride. You bring Wilson, and we'll sit near the water."

"Okay," Colleen agreed.

They met near the punts. There were flowers everywhere. They filled every nook and cranny of window boxes. They dripped from pots attached to streetlights, and lined the paths and sidewalks. They climbed up the riverbanks, and sprouted between patio bricks.

After lunch David said, "Amberjean, do you want to take a little walk?"

Amberjean replied, "I'd be happy to. Or would you rather take a boat ride? Have you ever been punting?"

David smiled. "No, but it looks like fun. Let's all go."

"Sure," Amberjean answered.

They went to an empty boat. David sat beside her. He turned toward her and quietly said, "When your grandparents died together, your grandmother's sewing basket was in a box sent to me, to keep for you. I took a quick look and put it in the attic. I didn't think of it until we made arrangements to meet here... then I went up to the attic and found the box. I thought you might like to have Mama Dot's sewing basket. But when I opened it, I found this.

"I haven't read it. But I think I know what it says. It's something your mother told me a long time ago." He paused. "It's for you, the way I believe it was meant to be—from your mother, to you alone."

David handed her a paper bag containing a small diary, covered in soft purple cloth with white flowers. It was locked, but a tiny key on a pink ribbon was tied to the closing flap.

Amberjean said, "Thank you," and started to take the book out of the bag, but then put it back in. "I'll look at it later."

"Good," David said. "You know how to reach me. I'll come to see you before I leave Scotland, if you like. Just be sure to let me know you're all right as you travel."

"I will, David. You can see I keep good company," Amberjean replied.

"I can. I'm impressed. Colleen is very level-headed, and you two look enough alike to be sisters."

"I know. I wish she played an instrument, then we could travel together. We really hit it off."

They watched the swans, and David enjoyed a tour of the campus before he left.

Colleen, Wilson, and Amberjean went back to her room for a glass of wine. "What did he give you?" they asked when they saw the bag.

"My mother's diary."

They were silent. "Did you know she had one?" Colleen asked.

"No."

"Do you want me to leave so that you can read it?" Wilson asked.

"Maybe we should both leave," Colleen said.

"No, I don't think so. I want to think about it, and talk about it, okay?" Amberjean answered.

"Sure. How old do you think she was when she wrote it?" Wilson asked.

"And how old was she when she had you? Does the front page have a date imprinted on it?" Colleen asked.

Amberjean opened the bag a little bit. She could see the date on the front.

1937

"Amberjean is going to find out who her dad is this afternoon," Colleen said.

"Maybe I'm not ready to know," Amberjean replied.

But before long, she was ready.

"I'm going to the library for a little while. Catch you later." She left with the diary in the bag.

Wilson turned to Colleen and took the pictures out of his briefcase again.

"I'll be out of the Navy in eighteen months," he said. "But I think I should buy the farm now. I can use my inheritance as the down payment, and ask the present owner to stay there as a tenant. He has mentioned his willingness to do that for a year or so. That way I can use the rent to make payments on the loan. What do you think?"

Colleen looked at him. "Think about what? Your marriage? Your potential divorce? A boy named True? Your relationship with a forty-five-year-old woman named sweet potato?"

Wilson smiled. "You have a way with a phrase."

"Let's just say you give a girl a lot to think about," Colleen continued.

"What about love?" he asked.

"What do you mean?" Colleen answered.

"What about the fact that I love you, and you love me?"

Colleen stood up and paced. "You never said it. I never said it. What makes you think it?"

He looked lost. "There's no other explanation. At first, I didn't know what it was."

Colleen was warming up. "When did you know? Before you got married, or after? Or when you got tired of sweet potatoes?"

Wilson was unsure. "Ahhhh."

At the library, Amberjean sought an empty window-alcove with a huge upholstered chair. She took the diary out of the bag, and held it on her lap for a moment. She couldn't remember being so nervous in her life. Her heart was pounding.

The only thing on the cover was a date... 1937.

This book belongs to: Adeline Frazier
Address: 49 Lone Pine Road Attleboro, Mass.
Phone: (Osborne) 25514

The first page was dated July 23, 1937.

Dear Diary,

I said good-bye to Mom and Dad and took the bus to Providence, changed to the Fall River line and walked from the station to Mrs. Joubert's rooming house, all by two p.m. They were going to drive me, but the tractor needed a part and there wasn't enough time for the drive, the repair, and the fieldwork. Dad would have lost the whole day. Tomorrow and the next day, it is supposed to rain. He had no choice.

I'm just like a farmer. All I talk about is the weather. No wonder I had to leave. I'm going to look for a job tomorrow and explore the city. I hope to make enough money to shop. I'm sick of homemade clothes.

Mrs. Joubert said I can clean the kitchen after supper in return for two meals a day. Things are going so well already. Coming here was a great idea.

July 26, 1937

Dear Diary,

Millie at the end of the hall took me with her to work. I already have a job at Anderson's Mill on New Bedford Street. Thank God! I don't have to wander from place to place looking. Millie told the floor manager I could work beside her, and she would show me the ropes. She is beautiful, someone I would never meet in Attleboro, and is only working until she meets a rich man. If she meets one, she plans to get pregnant, and marry him and live like a queen.

I know how bad that sounds, diary... that's why I will never say it to anyone else. But Millie says if a man thinks he is a father, he is inspired to buy a home and start a family. She says all men need a little push... like a baby needs a push to get up and walk... Mom told me I would miss Donald, even though a duck is a stupid pet, and she was right. I miss him a lot.

August 2, 1937

Dear Diary,

You would not believe how many dishes and pots they use to make supper here. Last night I was in the kitchen until ten p.m. I thought I would be there until morning wiping grease off the stove. Mrs. Joubert checks the kitchen before she lets me leave. She has a rear-end wider than the oven. Otherwise, I would have shoved her in it and turned the gas on. (just wishful thinking)

August 10, 1937

Dear Diary,

I just got paid for the first time and after I settled with Mrs. Joubert for my room and the lunches I pack to take to work, I was almost completely broke. I can't believe how much money disappears for an occasional trolley ride, soap, and socks and stuff. The city is for rich people. By the time I finish at the mill, walk home to save money, and eat supper, it is time to clean the kitchen. Sometimes I want to go home so bad, but I know Mom and Dad need the five dollars a week I will be sending. They are having a tough time too.

Millie wants me to go with her to a clambake next weekend.

August 19, 1937

Dear Diary,

Yesterday I went to the clambake with Millie and Frisco. It was the worst day of my life. It was so hot and humid I had a beer. And the beer was so good, I had another and I was so tired from working like a dog, I had one with supper. Anyway, that one made me sleepy. Frisco told me I should nap for an hour in the barn loft. He said no one would bother me and he would play cards downstairs so that he could keep an eye on the ladder to make sure.

I went up there and fell asleep like a stone. Then he came and lay down with me and woke me with his misbehavior. I am so sorry and ashamed. I was ready to scream when an earless boy came up the ladder and Frisco stopped, thank God. The boy jumped down the ladder, and Frisco followed.

In a few minutes, I went down, but Frisco was joking with the earless boy and didn't see me. I hate him. I sneaked away to find Millie and the girls from the mill. Like a dope, I had a few more beers with them before I tried to get the boat back to Fall River without telling anyone. I almost stepped on the earless boy on the beach. I fell on him and we both cried and then I started to comfort him. Before I knew it I had comforted him too much. He was so sad, and handsome, and pitiful, and crying so hard. I comforted him "completely," diary. I was drunk and now I am ruined.

When Amberjean got to October 12, she was stunned. "Oh my God!" she said.

October 12, 1937

Dear Diary,

My friend didn't come on September 2 and didn't come on October 2. I am sick all the time, and when Millie asked me if I was pregnant, I said No! But I know I am. I have to do something quick. I wish I were dead. I quit my job today! told my boss I had to go home because my mother was dying. That's not a lie; she will keel right over when I tell her. Then I told Mrs. Joubert I was leaving. Tomorrow is Saturday and I'm going home. I will take all my stuff with me, but God knows what I will do if they throw me out.

Amberjean closed the book and sat back to think. Colleen's mother, Marie, was Amberjean's mother's aunt. That made Colleen and Amberjean first cousins, once removed, on their mothers' side. This, they'd known all along.

But based on what she'd just read, the earless boy Amberjean's mother had been with at the clambake had to be Colleen's uncle, Padraig, the brother of Colleen's father, Edward.

So if Amberjean was Padraig's daughter, that would mean that on their fathers' side, she and Colleen were true first cousins!

Amberjean had been gone over an hour. She went back to the residence and knocked on Colleen's door. "What's going on in here?" she asked.

"Time for some battlefield medicine," Wilson said. "You look like you could use some." He filled small glasses with wine and served them.

Amberjean said, "Colleen, didn't you tell me that your grandfather held clambakes for mill workers?"

Colleen answered, "Yes."

Amberjean continued, "And your uncle Padraig worked at the clambakes?"

Colleen again said, "Yes."

"You have to read my mother's diary entry for August 19 and October 12. It seems that she met him at one of those clambakes."

Colleen carefully opened the book and read both entries. "Oh my God!" she whispered.

Amberjean said, "I want to know where he is, and if he's still alive. Let's call your mother."

They gathered as much change as they could, and went to find a pay phone.

Marie told them she was sure that she would have been notified if Padraig had died, and since she hadn't heard, she thought he was still at the Rose Laytham Nursing Home... and she gave them the phone number.

Amberjean was so jittery that Colleen had to place the call. "This is Padraig O'Leary's niece, and I'd like to know how my uncle is doing." The ward nurse assured her that he was alive... weak, but alive. Colleen did not want to go. She had just arrived in Cambridge, didn't have any money, and she barely knew her uncle.

But Amberjean *had* to go. "Even if it takes every nickel I'll ever have in my life, I have to go now, and I'll pay for both of us. You have to go with me... you are my family. My father doesn't even know he has a child, and I want to see him before he dies. I think he wants to meet me. Let's buy the tickets and go... right now. Please..."

Wilson went to the airport with them, and waved goodbye as they left on the first plane they could catch. In New York they got a train to Providence. From Providence they took the bus to Fall River. When they got to Padraig O'Leary's bedside in a long room of bedridden old men, his eyes were closed.

Colleen reached out and touched her uncle's arm. He looked at her, puzzled. She showed him an old dog-eared picture that she always carried with her. It was a favorite of hers because it showed the whole family. She was just a little girl in a black watch plaid dress, holding Sheila's hand, and standing in front of Marie and Edward. She pointed to herself and then to her father. Padraig's eyes flooded with tears as he realized who she was.

He pointed to Amberjean and then to Sheila in the picture. "No," Colleen said. "This is not Sheila."

Amberjean took her mother's picture out of the diary and handed it to Padraig. He looked at the picture of Adeline as a young woman and wept. He made noises that broke their hearts.

Then Amberjean took a picture from her wallet—a picture of her mother holding Amberjean when she was a baby. She pointed to the baby and said, "Me. Me. Me." Then she pointed to her heart. "Me. Me. Me," she said.

"Ou. Ou. Ou," he said.

She touched her heart and then his heart. Her heart... then his heart. "Me. Ou. Me. Ou."

Pulling her hair back, she showed him her ears. "Me. Ou." He reached out to touch one of them. She came closer and brought his hand to it.

Then she touched his ears, running her fingers down the bumpy ridges.

Padraig was crying. So were Colleen and Amberjean. They all laughed and cried at the same time. Marie and Edward arrived and Edward spoke to Padraig in the way they understood.

Later, Amberjean took out her guitar and played for her father. She sang every song she knew. Padraig fell asleep with a broad smile on his face. In his hand he held the picture of Adeline and Amberjean.

15 Padraig's Funeral

The funeral of Padraig O'Leary was a small gathering. Marie and Edward made a Clam Boil for the family—Amberjean, Colleen, Skinhead, Portuguese Pete, Charity, George, and Aunt Janet. Flo's Clam Shack in Island Park provided clam cakes and clam chowder.

At her first sight of Newport from the bridge coming into town, Colleen wept with gratitude for Newport, and her parents. Her eyes had seen bleak places where she longed for the colors of the ocean, the splendor of the waves, the sailboat races, the lobster boats heading toward the horizon, and coming into the harbor at the end of the day; the crashing waves, and screeching of birds fishing for supper... clanging channel markers, and the smell of salt spray. Every one of her senses was satisfied when she arrived home.

Padraig would have loved this gathering in his honor. Marie spoke of a time when they were young and Padraig used to dance with a broom. Edward took the broom away from him and continued to dance, throwing the broom back and forth until they had both fallen down. Sheila used to beg them to do the broom dance.

Colleen remembered the trip they took when she and Sheila were little. It was before Edward took the seat out, so he could carry barrels of bait, and the girls had the huge back seat of the old Plymouth to themselves. She remembered the joke Edward told Marie when he thought the girls were sleeping.

"There was a man and his wife riding in the car on a long trip and the woman wanted to stop to go to the bathroom. The man kept telling her to wait 'til the next town. But there weren't any nearby towns and eventually the wife said, 'Stop this car somewhere I can go to the bathroom, or I'm going to roll down the window and go!' The man said, 'There's no place to stop... do what you have to do!'

"They passed two men with hands held high, hitchhiking. One of the men sniffed his thumb, and said, 'I wonder kind of tobacco that guy was chewing?'

"The other said, 'I don't know, but you should have seen the jaws on him.'"

Those attending the funeral remembered that was the only joke Edward knew... he never told jokes since everything around him was a joke, like the time he bought a little goat and brought it in the livingroom when Marie's relatives arrived. It was outrageous and they laughed until their sides hurt. Then the others told their stories.

There was one about the time Edward dressed as Santa while all of Marie's family hung around the piano and played Italian folk songs. When one of the young cousins pulled Santa's beard off. Edward ran into the bathroom and all the little kids banged on the door.

The stories were of happy times, and crazy times, and it was a wonderful wake for everyone. All their sad and mad feelings were gone, and they were left with enough love for everyone, with some left over. And in that beautiful minute Edward and Marie forgave Charity and George.

More than six years earlier, Edward had seen a FOR SALE sign on a house in Island Park, and he took Marie to drive by it. Of course she loved it, but Edward would not let her call for information.

"It is important to wait until the people are anxious, and not so convinced about their price, whatever it is," he insisted.

They bickered about the house, walked around it, and rode by it when they went out for ice cream on the weekends.

When Charity and George came to visit, they showed them the house. George wanted to know what it cost, but Edward said, "It is too early to call...we're letting them get anxious."

The next time Edward and Marie rode by the house, the sign was gone. George's motorcycle was in the driveway, and Charity was standing near some boxes. Their smiles were so large you could see their tonsils.

Charity shouted, "Come see my new house!"

But Edward waved goodbye, and Marie pointed to her watch. They didn't see each other again until Padraig's wake.

George spoke first. He said, "Why didn't you stop that day?"

Edward said, "We didn't have time to chew the fat."

George said, "I understand, buddy, but I sure have missed you."

Edward said, "I know."

And everyone hugged everyone.

There is nothing like death to bring the Clan together. Amberjean played her guitar, Colleen played the piano, and the mourners sang Danny Boy. Padraig would have loved it all.

THE END

ACKNOWLEDGMENTS

Grateful acknowledgment is made to Professor Emeritus, J. Michael Lennon, for his mentorship and encouragement at Wilkes University Creative Writing Masters Program.

Thank you to Ann Feldmann's recollections of the New York Foundling Hospital. And to J. Patrick and Mary Ford for their memories of transatlantic flight, and to Leslie Spanik Cook, a rare friend from second grade until the present, who provided a quiet room with a comfortable chair many years ago when it seemed that the end of this story was in sight.

It is impossible to measure the gratitude I have for my parents. And my profound appreciation to the best brother in the world, my Irish twin, J. Barry O'Neill. The authenticity of his lobstering information was critical.

Thank you, most importantly, to my husband Jim, the love of my life, and most enthusiastic helpmate, supporter, and best friend for 58+ years. It is Jim and our children, who give me grace, and room to grow... Tamara, who was born to run the show; Jennifer, who always shows up and does more than expected; and Joe, who will always and forever be the missing part of us.

ABOUT THE AUTHOR

MAUREEN O'NEILL, the daughter of a lobsterman, grew up on an island fifteen miles long and five miles wide. At an early age, books convinced her that exotic places like Bali Ha'i were over the bridge and far away from Newport, Rhode Island. She married Jim Hooker, a naval officer, and they moved from the East Coast to the West Coast twice before settling in Northern Virginia with their children, Tammy, Joe, and Jennifer. They later relocated to North Carolina.

Cancer and heart failure opened doors she didn't know existed. On September 3, 2011, she received the gift of life, a heart transplant. Her first book, *Shelly's Heart*, chronicles her journey and the joy of its blessings. Her second book, *Forever in Our Hearts*, followed the death of her son, Joe, in 2018. Grief does not end; people endure.

Along the way from birth to the present, Maureen discovered that in her 81 years, she had never been anywhere as beautiful as Newport, R.I.

Clan of the Lobsterman was born of longing for her old home, where her mother sat on the front porch on summer nights because it was too hot and muggy to sleep. Hiding underneath that porch in the dark, Maureen listened to tall tales and scuttlebutt she didn't understand, and only half remembers. The oddball characters in this warm-hearted novel didn't die of old age; they disappeared when air conditioning killed porch-sitting and narrators stopped making up the characters she loved.

www.ingramcontent.com/pod-product-compliance
Lightning Source LLC
Chambersburg PA
CBHW020145120726
47903CB00007B/2417